WHAT SOME
WOULD CALL LIES

WHAT SOME WOULD CALL LIES

Novellas

by Rob Davidson

Five Oaks Press
FIVE-OAKS-PRESS.COM

ISBN: 978-1-944355-47-0

Originally published by Five Oaks Press
Reprinted by Formal Feeling Publishing

Cover Photo: Federica Campanaro, on Unsplash

Interior Layout: Lynn Houston

Author Photo: Sharon DeMeyer

Printed in the U.S.A.

Also by Rob Davidson

FICTION
Spectators: Flash Fictions
The Farther Shore
Field Observations

CRITICISM
The Master and the Dean: The Literary Criticism of
Henry James and William Dean Howells

For Linda

CONTENTS

Shoplifting, or, How Dialectical Materialism
    Can Change Your Life   11

Infidels   83

I tell what some would call lies. …For not only have I always had trouble distinguishing between what happened and what merely might have happened, but I remain unconvinced that the distinction, for my purposes, matters.

—Joan Didion, *Slouching Towards Bethlehem*

If personal memory is false, what happens when you try to construct a memory of something that, in fact, you do not remember, but should—that you desperately want to remember?

—Greil Marcus, "Tied to History"

SHOPLIFTING
or,
How Dialectical Materialism Can Change Your Life

1

Standing in the aisle of her local K-Mart, Monica Evans held up a toddler T-shirt for inspection. Every boy's shirt featured an image of a race car or a monster truck, a baseball player or a superhero. It seemed so primal. Like, get me a sharp stick and a loincloth, already! She wandered across to the girls' section. Here, everything was flowers and birds, yellows and pinks. Equally cliché, she knew, but if you must live your life as a cliché you could at least choose lavender.

Browsing, she found the cutest flower-print dress, sized for an eighteen-month-old. And it was on mega-reduction. She hesitated, thinking of what her husband would say.

Nothing a sharp riposte couldn't tame. Into the cart it went.

Jacob began squirming in his baby seat. The little guy was probably hungry. "Almost bottle time," Monica cooed, hoping to soothe him. At the sound of the magic B-word he let out a yelp and began thrashing as if stung by a bee. In a moment of poor judgment, Monica unstrapped him and set him on the floor. Immediately, Jacob took off. She caught up with him two aisles later, in the toys. With what could only be described as animal ferocity, the child ripped items off the shelves faster than his mother could replace them. Finally, she scooped him up and quickly made her way to the checkout line, leaving the toy aisle looking like a tornado had hit it. Jacob wriggled and writhed, a yellow stuffed animal, a giraffe or something, firmly in his mitt. She planned to rip it out of his hands at the last possible moment. Yet by the time they'd made it through the check-out line, he wasn't holding it. Unceremoniously dropped, she'd assumed, somewhere along the way.

Later that afternoon, Monica dug a hand into her shoulder bag, rooting after one of Jacob's pacifiers, and there, wedged between a spare diaper and her copy of James Frey's *A Million Little Pieces*, she found Henry the Hammer: a plush, stuffed toy, golden yellow, with fawn-like eyes on either side of its head and a distended, goofy grin on its neck. Surprised, she held it before her like some Egyptian artifact.

"Hammah!" Jacob shouted, hurtling across the room like a troglodyte, arms outstretched. Before Monica knew it, Jacob had grabbed Henry the Hammer and was merrily thumping away on the hardwood floor of the family's living room. She was quite content to let him continue. She knew she had not paid for Henry the Hammer. Her son had stolen it. Unwittingly, mind you. But a theft had occurred, and she was technically an accomplice.

Her first thought was to return the toy with an apologetic explanation. Surely Jacob was not the first toddler to stuff something surreptitiously into his mother's purse. Or, she could fork over the money and keep the kid happy. The price tag dangled from the end of the toy on a little plastic hoop. She wondered how much Henry cost. But with Jacob joyfully pounding away, Monica wasn't about to interrupt. She wanted five minutes of peace. Just five minutes. If those five minutes were the product of unethical or illegal behavior, so be it.

Quietly, she stepped into the kitchen and fixed herself a cup of tea. She picked up her copy of *A Million Little Pieces*, which she was re-reading after having watched Oprah scold its author for falsifying certain episodes from his past. Seeing Frey cower under his hostess's onslaught, watching him apologize and back down had made Monica so angry she actually threw a Nerf ball at the television, screaming "Plead your genre!" Herself the author of a partially-completed memoir, she knew something about being attacked. A month ago, she'd mailed the first four chapters of her opus-in-progress to her mother in Indianapolis. Claudia had phoned not to praise her daughter's eloquence or her gift for characterizing her beloved but departed sister, Saundra, but to accuse her of stealing from the dead.

"It was your sister who got lost at the Tippecanoe County Fair in 1974, not you," Claudia said.

They argued about that for a while. Monica was convinced that it was she who'd found herself stranded, alone on the midway, clutching a tower of pink cotton candy in one hand and a stuffed penguin in the other. It was she who'd broken down in tears, wailing as only an abandoned six-year-old can: hopelessly, existentially lost.

Claudia challenged her on that, too, insisting that a six-year-old cannot suffer an existential dilemma. Monica said it's all relative. What's existential when you're six would only be a temporary annoyance when you're sixteen. And the existential dilemmas of sixteen-year-olds are, of course, completely laughable. But Claudia Barnes, Ph.D., Doctor of Ethics and Philosophy for All Time, whipped out some textbook definition of existentialism, citing Kierkegaard, Nietzsche, and Sartre.

"Bo-ring!" blurted Monica. "Words like 'existential' start out specific, but eventually become generalized. They get appropriated, colloquialized. That's when *ordinary* people start to use them. Like when you call your grocer a fascist."

"I would never call my grocer that," retorted Claudia. "That's hyperbole, and it's worse than wrong, it's dangerous. You're devaluing the term. Save a word like 'fascist' for when you really need it."

"But my grocer *is* a fascist. Do you know what a gallon of organic milk costs?"

"Why steal your sister's memories, anyway?" Claudia finally asked. "You're twenty-seven and the mother of a toddler. You've done things. You were in that band. You've had a kid. You almost finished your M.F.A. Good grief, you grew up in Indiana, the most conservative state in the nation, and now you live in California, the most liberal. You have plenty to write about."

"Ha! That just shows what you know," Monica snapped. And she explained to her mother how, once you moved inland from the coast, northern California was essentially a Republican stronghold. "Chico is a little hamlet of progressive thought surrounded by a wasteland of backwater conservatism," she concluded.

"Great! Write about that!" Claudia fired back. "But leave your sister alone."

You'll just get it wrong, Monica thought, silently completing her mother's argument for her, *like you always do.*

"We were sisters, Mom. I grew up with her. I don't see how I can write a memoir of my childhood and not write about her."

Claudia didn't know what to say to that, so she simply repeated her request before saying good-bye.

Monica stood in the middle of the room, phone in hand, for a long moment before dropping the phone into its cradle. It answered with a sharp beep. Monica shot the phone a quick middle finger, cursing her mother for the millionth time and wishing, for the billionth time, that her sister were still alive. *She* would've laughed and found the mistake funny. She would've told Monica not to worry, to go ahead and keep it that way. To just keep writing. Saundra believed in people. If you said you wanted to be a writer, then that's what she wanted you to be. Saundra did not trot out old mistakes and remind you of them every chance she got. Saundra did not sit in quiet judgment, a scorn fueled by bitterness and unreconciled loss.

Monica understood she'd made a mistake in showing her work to her mother. Of *course* her mother was going to show resistance. That was Claudia! What Monica needed to do was take a deep breath and start again. Ignore her mother, that naysayer. That critic. Few people on earth are more oriented toward dissecting the flaws in others—while demonstrating a remarkable inability to train the microscope on one's self—than the professor of philosophy.

There was another, subtler issue that perplexed Monica, and that was the question of how she had mistakenly appropriated Saundra's experience. Memories of early childhood are fluid, of course, as likely to be the product of a parent's repeated storytelling as an actual memory of the event. But to substitute yourself for your sister? And to believe whole-heartedly that it had happened to you? That was *spooky*. Almost like somebody planted it there. Almost like her sister wanted her to remember the scene for her.

There was no question about it: she would keep writing. She just needed to focus, to concentrate, to apply herself. And so Monica, sitting in her kitchen in a patch of late afternoon sunlight, made two resolutions. First, to return to her manuscript. Second and most importantly, to write what seemed true and then to hold her ground, no matter what anyone said.

"Hammah!" cried Jacob, running through the room, waving his newest toy. His eyes blazed with the unmitigated pleasure of total, uncontested ownership, a joy known only to toddlers and certain obscure, eastern European dictators.

Resolution number three: return Henry the Hammer to his rightful home.

Monica did not return Henry the Hammer. Soon her husband Jeff was home and it was time to think about cooking dinner and bathing the baby before putting him down for bedtime. Next thing she knew, it was nine o'clock and all she wanted to do before collapsing into bed was clean up the apocalypse of toys strewn in every conceivable corner of the living room. She enlisted Jeff's help, and it was he who bent down to pick up Henry the Hammer. "You forgot to clip off the price," he said, twiddling the white cardboard tag with a finger. And then, in an instant, he snapped the plastic hoop and tossed the tag in the trash. The toy went into a plastic bucket, promptly buried beneath a dozen other toys.

That might have been the end of it, but when Monica saw the toy the next day, her conscience was pricked, however lightly. Yes, she should've paid for it. It wasn't Jacob's, when you got right down to it. But then it was only an over-priced bit of stuffed polyester. Nothing truly valuable. Come to think of it, charging six bucks for that piece of crap was highway robbery. It'd probably been assembled by a starving child in southeast Asia working fourteen hours a day in a sweatshop. Stealing the damn thing was almost a form of protest.

She knew stealing was wrong. It's a lesson every child learns, one way or another. As a kid, she'd never stolen much. But her late sister Saundra— well, that was a different matter entirely. Yes, Saundra, the hotshot lawyer, Momma's golden child with the full ride to law school, Miss Jr. Ethics and Philosophy for All Time, yes, *that* Saundra had had a little streak of trouble in her early teens. Saundra and her friends had taken to stealing make-up and jewelry from local department stores. They'd started out with plastic trinkets and junk, slowly working their way up to silver and name-brand items. Then came the fateful day when Saundra tried to walk out of a store wearing a pair of brand new Ray-Bans. She was stopped at the door and rather roughly pushed into the manager's office, where she was read the riot act and threatened with arrest. By the time their mother had arrived to rescue the poor thing, Saundra was hysterical, convinced that she was going to be led off to prison in chains. This man so terrified her that for years to come she would not step foot in that store—wouldn't even go near the mall where it was located. Claudia toyed with the idea of suing for some kind of mental abuse. But the family should have been grateful. Whatever that ape of a manager had said to Saundra, it cured her of a bad habit. And it probably changed the course of her life. Everybody knows the best priests were hell raisers in their youth; it follows that petty thieves make the best lawyers. They know their kind.

After Saundra's death Monica froze up. She dropped out of the M.F.A. program at Indiana, yes, but it wasn't sheer laziness, as her mother intoned. Rather, she'd taken the university's kind offer of a grief waiver and dropped her spring classes. She'd intended to return, but summer turned into fall, fall into winter. She slept late, shuffled around her apartment in a daze, her mind foggy and aching, her body exhausted. Like a prolonged hangover. It was an era she'd just as soon forget.

Then she'd suddenly, unexpectedly met Jeff Evans, a computer engineering student in his final year of graduate school, a man who, despite being a total computer geek, was not haplessly introverted and anti-social. He liked martinis and T.C. Boyle; he liked long hikes through the hills of Brown County with a bottle of Rioja and a wedge of manchego cheese stashed in his rucksack; and he looked *good* with his shirt off. Best of all, he understood her fear and depression and anxiety and was patient with her mourning and loved her through it, during it, and, she now thought, perhaps because of it. So that when she found herself suddenly, unexpectedly pregnant and Jeff suddenly, unexpectedly proposed to her, she agreed. Two months later, he finished his degree and landed a promising job with an internet startup in northern California, and Monica found herself living on the West Coast, a grad school dropout and the stay-at-home mother of a newborn. In the space of two years, her entire life had been torn apart, turned inside-out, upended and rear-ended, demolished and mysteriously replenished. Honestly, it was enough to make a girl bonkers.

In graduate school, Monica had written short stories. She'd wanted to be the next Lorrie Moore: wry and witty, but also smart and deep. The call to memoir was recent and unexpected. It had started several months earlier, when she began to see a therapist, Dr. Bellegarde. He was a large, avuncular man with an office in downtown Chico. The room was oddly shaped like a slice of pie, with a single large window that looked out on a parking lot and a trash bin. Monica sat on an overstuffed leather couch that gave an exasperating sigh every time she sat on it. Monica had gone to Dr. Bellegarde concerned that, nearly three years after Saundra's death, she still hadn't come to terms with it. She thought about it frequently. Shouldn't she have put it behind her by now? Bellegarde had encouraged her to talk about it there in his office, so she did.

Saundra had left work on a Thursday evening, around seven o'clock at night. She'd met a girlfriend at a bar downtown for dinner and a drink, though that quickly turned into several drinks for Saundra, who freely admitted she was in a funk. She'd flunked the Illinois bar exam earlier that year, and though she had a promising job with a law office in Chicago—a firm willing to keep her around while she prepared a second attempt—she wasn't feeling confident about anything. The stress of working full time while studying was wearing her down. She couldn't sleep. And to cap it all off, her boyfriend—who'd passed the bar on his first try, a year earlier—had recently moved an hour away, out into the suburbs, to step into his uncle's lucrative law office, which he would eventually take over. Yes, Mark Schultz had been handed a golden ticket.

Saundra, deep into her third martini, had started weeping. Ann, the friend, consoled her. She got them out of there and hired a cab to take Saundra up to Evanston. What you need, Ann had told her, is a good night's sleep. Putting her in that cab, sending her off alone, Ann said she'd felt worried. Saundra wasn't usually like that, so brittle and worn.

The next morning, Mark phoned Saundra at her office, thinking of tweaking their dinner plans. A few hours later, when he'd gotten no return call, he telephoned her supervisor. Saundra hadn't come in that day, hadn't called in sick, they didn't know where she was. Very uncharacteristic. There was no answer at her apartment in Evanston, nor on her cell. Mark raced to her apartment and he was the one who found her in bed, seemingly asleep. The autopsy indicated a toxic mix of alcohol and prescription sleeping pills.

Her sister had been depressed, no doubt about that. But had she been suicidal? There was no note. She'd never mentioned killing herself. And, frankly, it just wasn't like her. But Ann, the girlfriend she'd met the night before, had clearly been concerned. Mark knew that Saundra had been down—really, really down after failing the bar. More than she was letting on. Even Monica, her estranged sister, knew that Saundra had been struggling. So, no one could totally rule out a suicide.

"That's what torments me, I guess," Monica told Dr. Bellegarde. "Whatever was going on in my sister's head. Nobody really knows. Maybe she just screwed up and popped one too many pills after one too many martinis. But what if it wasn't an accident? What if she got home that night and just felt beyond horrible? What if she broke and did something impulsive?"

Either scenario seemed equally plausible—and implausible. Monica simply didn't know, but she felt she *must* know. And if she can't know it, she said, she must imagine it.

Bellegarde asked if she'd tried writing it down.

"You mean for you to read?"

"If you want. But I probably won't need to. You're not writing it for me, after all."

"So why am I paying you?"

Bellegarde had laughed at that, all Falstaff and beer. He cheered her up, she could say that much.

Then the doctor had grown serious. Monica wanted the facts because she wanted closure, he said. As long as there were unanswered questions, she wouldn't have closure. She must accept that she would never know more than she did at that moment. That wasn't going to change. Bellegarde wanted to work with her on grieving strategies, finding ways to move forward. Imagining the death scene, entertaining speculations and suppositions, was one step in the process, he said, but it wouldn't be enough. She must move beyond it.

"We'll take it one step at a time," he'd concluded. "You go home and write down whatever you need to write down, and next week we'll see where you're at."

And so, a few days later, Monica sat down at her laptop and opened up her word processor. The cursor blinked patiently in the upper left-hand corner of the empty screen. She sat for several minutes, her fingers frozen. Then she remembered a writing exercise from an old creative writing class—a five minute freewrite, no editing. Just type two pages, get black on white. Monica took a deep breath and began.

* * *

Mornings, before school, Saundra often sat before the tri-fold mirror in their mother's bedroom, brushing and then braiding her own hair. Monica sat on the large, king-sized bed behind Saundra, fascinated by her sister's slow, careful gestures. She was so patient and precise, staring at herself in the mirror, dead-on, self-absorbed. Her braids always came out perfectly matched.

That was Saundra in a nutshell. At the playground, she preferred swings to slides, climbing bars to sand boxes. In high school, she wore slacks, skirts, pants suits. She lettered in swimming; edited the senior yearbook; was elected President of the Debate Club. No one was surprised when she won a scholarship to the University of Chicago. Law school at Northwestern followed, and she landed an internship with a distinguished law firm inside the Loop. She worked twelve, fourteen hours a day. Six days a week. They loved her drive, her tenacity, her good spirits. There was talk of finding her a position after she passed the state bar.

Then Saundra died.

Monica wasn't sure why the mystery of her sister's death bothered her so much. It haunted her, the not-knowing. It felt like an empty circle asking to be colored in. The idea of writing about it felt good and helpful. She would be re-creating her sister—and herself. There were two sisters waiting to be constructed in words. Two sisters not so much lost as waiting to be found, waiting to be made anew. Saundra's death might not be an end so much as a beginning: an event that begged for a context, a conclusion in need of the story preceding it.

Monica's first essay attempt failed, but for an interesting reason. She wrote one prosaic page about the death before hitting hard return and launching into an associated memory, a long-buried anecdote about riding around in the back of a pick-up truck one summer with Saundra and their cousins, Dylan and Danny, drinking half-warm beer in cans and doing fishtails and the like. Typical teen pranks. The boys had tried to kiss them, but they were their cousins! Nothing doing!

That essay—just a sketch, really—came out pretty well. Or at least it was the first piece of writing in a long time that it felt good to write. Monica thought it showed some promise, so she continued to work on it. And then another, similar piece: an essay about a girls' club that she and Saundra had formed one summer. Though the club had no clear mission, they'd designed uniforms and invented a complex initiation ritual that frightened off the one girl they'd managed to recruit.

Monica loved writing that piece, unearthing the long-buried memories, the happy stuff. For once, she wasn't stopping at the bottom of every page, banging her head against the computer keyboard. She kept at it, and the words, the memories, kept coming. Oh, if only her mother knew how to read! Because the essay about being lost at the fair was the best one. She'd recorded every detail: the hard, bright lights of the midway; flies buzzing around the wire-frame garbage can; the red, white and blue tracks of the giant slide, children descending on burlap sacks, screaming with glee while she stood there suddenly looking left, looking right, looking behind—her parents, her sister, all vanished. She called their names, her words vanishing into a throng of people: strangers stuffing their faces with corn dogs; children with balloons and enormous stuffed pink elephants, their happiness now an affront. She bolted into the maze of bodies with no sense of direction, driven only by a sickening sting of panic. She finally stopped near the horse stables, the earthy smell of manure hovering in the air like a foreign perfume. It was a part of the fair she'd never seen, had never even known existed. And like a black wave it hit her: that slow, gnawing feeling of stark, unvarnished fear. She was lost. Abandoned. Forsaken.

It was, she had written, the moment that prepared her for her sister's death. From the initial panic, to the wash of terror and tears, to the inevitability of some stranger's kindness intervening in her plight, to the gradual understanding of her true situation and, eventually, its resolution, Monica had learned that people survive things; that fear eventually gives way to a kind of acceptance, however fragile; and that you're never so lost that someone won't find you, eventually.

If what she'd written wasn't factually true, she knew it was true in some other way. It was true for the narrator on the page, the character speaking to the reader. It had certainly become true for the author. She concluded that, in a way, the event had happened to her because she *had* written it, entered into it, taken a kind of possession of it. In a memoir, emotional truth trumped the facts. It led to a kind of higher truth. You were after art, that airy abstraction, that mirage.

This was the Truman Capote of *In Cold Blood*. This was the James Frey of *A Million Little Pieces*, even if the bastard couldn't own up to it. Go to hell, Oprah!

In a funny way that she wasn't entirely sure how to feel about, Monica believed she'd been granted a kind of permission to steal her sister's memory. Her mistake might not have been a mistake at all. Maybe, just maybe, Saundra *wanted* Monica to write the passage that way, in the first person, as if it had really happened to her. To write, if you like, her sister's autobiography for her.

The book would be a memoir of her sister's childhood, the life they shared in suburban Indiana: early childhood, adolescence, and those heady teenage years. Stories of their vacations in French Lick, boating on Patoka Lake, and kissing boys in Baden Springs. This would not be the Indiana of Dan Quayle or the Indy 500. There would be no hicks in the woods, no campy odes to corn. This would be a book of pastoral green hills; the incomparable beauty of Brown County State Park on a damp, misty morning in late autumn; of delicate first snows in December; of summer sunsets over the White River, the air thick with humidity. This would be *that* Indiana, a land few outsiders knew or understood.

It would be the story of two young girls growing up, two sisters joined at the hip. Two girls destined to break away from one another, to go their own ways, and yet to maintain an unspoken bond that transcended everything.

2

Monica and Jeff lived in a canyon twenty-five miles outside of Chico, California, their small home nestled in a grove of towering valley oaks and cedars overlooking Yolo Creek. Previous owners had built additions to the house on an as-needed basis, with a design sense that could only be called whimsical. The result was an odd mish-mash of styles with a quirky charm. Nothing matched. The oldest rooms had single-pane weighted windows; the most recent addition had double-paned vinyl coated windows that slid horizontally on tracks. One wing had clapboard siding and a steeply-pitched roof; another had pine boards and a flat roof. Over the years, the house had settled, shifting the oldest doorways at odd angles so that doors had to be planed to fit. There was no central hallway, just a succession of rooms built off the central living room, one room giving way into the other, often with uneven steps up or down between rooms. When they'd bought the place, three years ago, Jeff had spent a month painting each room a different color. Plum for their bedroom, avocado green in the sun room. Jeff's home office was a meditative blue. The baby's room was canary yellow, full of energy and action. Almost every room had a view of the creek. There was nothing Monica liked more than hearing the gentle burble of water in the quiet moments of a day, or in the stillness of the night.

The house had noises of its own. The wooden floors creaked and sighed under their feet. Monica had grown accustomed to most of these noises. She knew which boards in the living room groaned, which door hinges whined. On a windy day, the blinds rattled in the breeze, or the bedroom door might suddenly slam shut if she'd forgotten to wedge the doorstop underneath. She knew the sound of squirrels darting across the eaves, their tiny feet oddly resonant inside the house.

One day, as she was sitting in the living room with Jacob, pushing felt animals around in circles and naming things for him—*donkey, elephant, tiger*—she heard footsteps in the back of the house, the tread of bare feet in one of the back rooms. A small spike of adrenaline prickled across her neck and shoulders. Jeff was at work. Their closest neighbor lived a quarter of a mile down the road. Really, there was no one out there. But you never knew.

Curious, Monica walked through the baby's room, plunking little Jacob in his crib, and moved towards the back of the house. Just off the sun room was Jeff's study, a narrow room added on where the baby's room and the sun room met. The only way to see in there was to walk through the doorway between the two larger rooms. And when she did, she thought she glimpsed someone moving away from the doorway, out of view—just the back of a shoulder and part of the upper arm, wearing a yellow blouse. Just that narrow glimpse.

Immediately, her heart began to drum. But she boldly popped her head in the room and uttered a brisk, "Hello? Who's there?"

The room was empty. There was the old couch, covered in Jeff's computer manuals and piles of paper. The wooden table he used as a desk, a couple of chairs and a lamp. Bookshelves. The window was fastened shut. There was no other door, no way out. It must've been a trick of the light. Or too much high-test coffee that morning. She felt jittery, though she hadn't felt like that just prior.

A patch of sunlight brightened on the floor, then faded.

She smiled. You're talking to the walls now, she told herself. Senile at twenty-seven. Nice! She closed the door to the study and returned to her child.

A few days later, she heard the noise again, distinct and unmistakable: the pad of bare feet on wooden floors. A sound she lived with, a sound she heard every day. And yet somehow timid, hesitant. The sound of someone creeping about, trying not to call attention to herself, a guilty party caught in the act. Again, she went to check the room, and again she saw just that slender slice of the body, the upper shoulder and arm, the yellow blouse: a woman (she felt sure it was a woman) moving into the room, moving away from her.

The kitchen was narrow and tight, like a ship's galley. Just room for one knife-wielding chef. There, Monica prepared her share of the evening's dinner: a rice pilaf with stir-fried vegetables. Perspiration beaded across her brow. A pot rattled on the stovetop behind her as she chopped a carrot.

Jeff was grilling lamb shoulder chops on the Weber, which meant he could afford to sit on a stool at the narrow bar separating the living room from the kitchen, nursing a beer. Behind him, in the living room, Jacob sat on the floor pushing blocks around and thumping things with Henry, his beloved hammer. He wore a wonderful floral-print dress Monica had scored on a sale rack at the mall, a real steal.

"A little boy wearing a dress is not normal, that's all," Jeff said.

Monica turned to adjust the gas beneath the boiling water, the blue ring of light diminishing, tapering into a fine halo. "Ernest Hemingway's mother put him in a dress. It was normal then, when boys were very young. I can show you the picture. It's in Kenneth Lynn's biography." She chopped off the tip of a carrot with her knife. "Hemingway was plenty macho, if that's what you're worried about."

"Hemingway shot himself."

"But not because his mother made him wear a dress."

"Don't be so sure," he muttered. "Anyway, that was a hundred years ago. Today, in the twenty-first century, it's not normal."

"Says who?" She took a sip of wine. "Jacob's two. He's not a *boy* yet."

Jeff laughed. "You make it sound vile."

Monica looked down to the chopping board. She rubbed her finger along the carrot she was about to peel, feeling the bumpy, rough outer surface. Her peeler was old and bent, with a spot of rust on the handle. She made mental note to get a new one.

"You wanted a girl," he said. "We could try for another."

Monica shook her head. "No thanks. I've got my hands full with one."

"It won't always be like this."

"Easy for you to say. You're not home with him all day. Alone. In a valley thirty minutes from the nearest Starbucks."

She held his gaze as she brought her wine glass slowly to her mouth. It was an old discussion, occasionally an argument, currently on ice, the marital equivalent of trench warfare. She wanted to move into town; he didn't. One reason was the money, the other the simple fact that Jeff loved living in the country. For him, a long walk through a meadow with his toddler in a backpack was a grand day out. He liked tending to his vegetable garden, tinkering with the house, or trapping vermin in the attic. He liked seeing the stars at night, and hopping into the creek on a hot summer's day. He liked being cut off, a hermit. Monica had thought she would like it, too. But when the closest video rental shop carries only VHS in yellowing plastic boxes, or when all of your neighbors drive enormous white pick-up trucks with mud all over the side panels, or when all of your local road signs have been peppered by shotgun discharge, a girl just has to speak up.

"You used to like it out here," Jeff said. "It was a paradise."

"Don't you think people in heaven are bored out of their skulls? That's why we see ghosts. They want to be here, in the real world."

Jeff shot her a puzzled look. "Who sees ghosts?"

"Lots of people," Monica said, grabbing a slice of yellow pepper from the pile and crunching on it. "I know you're worried about the money, but

23

think about it. We take a wash on this house. So what? That's capitalism in a nutshell, isn't it? Buyers and sellers out to top one another. Somebody has to get shafted. Who cares?"

Jeff frowned. "If we lose money on this place, how do we afford a down payment on the next one?"

"People find ways. It's like jumping into a cold lake. Before you hit the water, you think it's going to kill you. But once you're in, you adjust pretty quickly. You recover."

Jeff took a long pull from his beer. "You're no economist."

Monica tossed a handful of chopped carrot into the sauce pot. "I want to live in town so we can be close to each other. Me, you. I want your office five minutes from home. I want a grocery store five minutes away, so if I forget Gorgonzola cheese, like I did today, I can pop out and get it. I want to be five minutes from the post office and the shopping mall and the stores that sell candy bars and *People* magazine. Don't you see? I want a five-minute lifestyle."

"Oh, now I get it," he said, slapping his forehead. "You're a Californian! Finally!"

She handed him a slice of sweet, crisp red pepper. "In life you're allowed to rewrite the script in the middle of a scene. We shouldn't trick ourselves into thinking we have to stay here, not if we want to leave."

Jeff popped the pepper slice in his mouth and chewed it slowly. "Maybe the scene doesn't need to be re-written. Maybe it's okay as it is. Maybe the trick is learning to accept it."

"But how do you know."

"I don't know. I just believe. I trust. I do the best I can with what I've got."

She gave him a long, hard stare. "Go check the meat, grillmeister."

Jeff glanced at his wristwatch, then bound out the door. Monica wiped clean her hands and went into the next room. Jacob sat on the floor, thumping the roof of a toy car. Monica knelt next to him and planted a kiss on his chubby, round cheek. Jacob smiled. A dress strap had fallen down one arm. Monica reached over and lifted it up onto his little shoulder.

"Pretty dress," she said. "Can you say, 'Pretty dress'?"

"Hammah!" he said, holding up the golden toy.

She heard the now-familiar creak of a board from the back of the house, the faint sound of a footstep falling. She held her breath, considering whether she would give in and look again.

Jeff came in bearing an empty platter. "Meat's not ready."

She stood. "Go into the back room right now."

He set the platter on the dining table. "What?"

24

"Honey, please." She put a hand on his forearm. "Walk back to your office and look. I heard something."

Their eyes met for a long moment.

"All right," he said, and walked towards the back of the house.

Monica tapped a finger against her lips, waiting. When he returned, he said he'd found nothing.

"What did you hear?" he asked.

"A bump. Maybe something fell off a shelf." She reached a finger up behind her ear, fidgeted with her hair. "Did you, like, *feel* anything back there?"

"Yeah. I felt hungry." He grabbed his beer off the counter and drained it.

"Don't think I'm crazy."

"About what?"

She told him she'd been hearing the footsteps, the groan of the floor. And every time she went to check, she saw that woman's shoulder in a yellow shirt, or a dress.

"I think this house might be h-a-u-n-t-e-d," she said, spelling it out for fear of frightening Jacob.

Jeff smiled. "So you're the one seeing g-h-o-s-t-s. Well, is it a friendly one?"

"I don't know."

"Ask next time." And then he scooped up Jacob from the floor and headed off to the bathroom to wash hands.

Monica didn't know if she should feel silly or scared, disturbed or delighted. She didn't believe in ghosts, not really. As a girl, she'd read books about poltergeists and hauntings. She'd played Ouija board with her sister and her girlfriends, held mock séances. They'd spooked themselves silly a few times, but Monica never took it seriously. It was just for a laugh, a bunch of hokum. Somehow, whatever was happening in her own house felt different. It felt, well, *real*. She didn't *think* she was making it up. She didn't *feel* crazy.

Okay, she felt a little crazy. But not delusional crazy. Not, you know, *crazy*-crazy.

She didn't know who or what it was, or what it meant. She only knew that it had to mean something. It was an image, a sound, a moment asking to be put in a context: a character looking for her story.

Later, in bed, Jeff wanted to make love. Their lovemaking had fallen into a kind of predictable, choreographed set of moves. A bit of kissing, some fondling, then the deed itself. Then Jeff would climb atop her as she lay on her back, spread out beneath him. Monica, not feeling especially turned on, concentrated on the sight of Jeff's bare chest looming over her. She ran her fingers up and down his finely-toned arms as he thrust in the familiar, rocking and sinuous motion they enjoyed. Jeff had always been lean and wiry, he was just lucky that way.

When he finished, he pulled out of her, then slid his thigh up against her crotch. She rarely climaxed with him inside her, and she'd taught him to let her rub up against his thigh until she had her orgasm. But that night, after a couple of minutes, she knew it wasn't going to happen. She tapped him gently on the hip, her signal for him to roll off. He collapsed into a heap beside her. Monica lay quietly beside him, naked, feeling his warmth dripping out of her, making its way down the innermost fold of her thigh to the bedsheets. She ran a hand over her belly, pinching at the extra skin there. Since having the baby, she'd put on twenty pounds, much of which she'd kept. She was bigger than she wanted to be, bigger than she'd ever been. This, despite her walks, her yoga, and various failed diets. She didn't know how to lose it, exactly. It was as if her body had betrayed her, as if she'd become another woman, someone she didn't recognize or understand or want to be.

After a quick trip to the bathroom to clean herself up, she and Jeff lay beside one another, arms and legs entwined. Usually, they lay like that until they both drifted off to sleep in that post-coitus, dreamy state of exhaustion that Monica loved so much. But that night, she couldn't lie still, and kept rolling over, moving Jeff's hands from one part of her body to another.

"Why so fidgety," he murmured.

"Who do you think she is?"

"Who?"

"The ghost."

"How do you know it's a woman?"

She traced her finger up and down his forearm. "I can tell."

She changed position, lifted her face up to his. "When I go in there, looking for her, I'm overcome with anxiety."

"You're freaking yourself out," he said.

"No, it's not like that. It's more like… she wants something."

"Unfinished business," he muttered. A minute later he'd fallen off, lightly snoring, his cheek warm against her shoulder.

It's me, Monica thought. She wants something from me.

3

Jeff worked for a small but growing internet startup. The founder, Martin Ramsey, had vision and ambition but proved thin on follow-through. That was where Jeff came in: a programmer who could translate Martin's ideas into a working, functional website. One such idea, a social networking site, had garnered interest by a larger firm in San Jose. After sniffing around the project for several weeks, the firm made an offer. The terms of the final sale specified various refinements in the service, all of which needed to be in place by late summer.

The reprogramming and expansion of the site proved more difficult than anticipated. It became clear that Martin's people and the people in San Jose needed to work face-to-face, and so Martin asked Jeff to go down for a few days. Then a week. Then another week. Now, in early April, it was a rare week that Jeff was in Chico. He left early Monday morning and drove into San Jose, returning home late Friday.

Monica tried to remain cheerful. Martin's business was growing, newly flush with cash. He'd given Jeff a healthy raise and, of course, covered his travel expenses. Martin had grand designs for his next project, which would entail a massive expansion of his company. There was talk of an eventual IPO, and a promotion for Jeff.

Monica knew this was good, and she shared in Jeff's excitement. He was so deeply invested in what he was doing that she was content to listen to his Saturday morning recap of the week's ups and downs not because she really cared about Java Script, P2P networks, or how to monitor user preferences, but because when Jeff talked about that stuff she saw the boy in his heart: his enthusiasm and conviction, his faith and optimism. That was the Jeff she loved, and the man she'd married.

She just wished she had that man around a little more often.

For Monica, the weekdays and weeknights grew longer and longer. All Jacob, all day, all the time. She did what she could to get out of the house, to feel like she had some community. They had their playgroup days, when she could sit in a room with half-a-dozen other stay-at-home moms and swap war stories. There was story time at the public library. There were the playgrounds and city parks, and the requisite field trips to the grocery store or the bank. And her beloved shopping mall, cathedral of high material culture, which Monica strolled through in air-conditioned comfort, her child strapped in his stroller, under the glass-shielded atriums filled with fake plastic trees and faux ivy. Monica did her share of shopping, mostly culling through the sales racks and clearances. When she found a bargain she couldn't live without, she bought it. But the mall was more than a place to shop. It was a place to have fun. She could plunk Jacob in a little space shuttle that lifted itself up and down, with flashing lights and a soft buzzing sound. Then there was the carousel, which Jacob absolutely adored, and every eleventh ride was free! Yes, when downtown held no charms, when the playgroups had disbanded, when it was just too damn hot to be outside, there was always the mall: a garden filled with unattractive people and beautiful things.

And, on the days when she couldn't bear the thirty-minute drive into Chico, there were the long hours at home in Yolo Canyon. She and Jacob kept plenty busy with their early morning walks (before it got too hot), with their playtime and story time and TV time. There were meals to eat, diapers to change, tears to dry. And there was one blessed nap every afternoon, two hours when Monica had a little time to herself.

With Jeff gone, that usually meant a whirlwind of cleaning: laundry, kitchen, garbage. Maybe a quick round of email. Time to write had all but evaporated. Monica tried to get up early, to have an hour or two before Jacob woke. Sometimes this worked, sometimes it didn't. Half the time she was too exhausted to drag herself out of bed. As the de facto solo parent, she'd given up putting Jacob to bed in his crib; she kept him in bed with her, where they snuggled and spooned all night. Jacob was a little heat-seeking missile, and when Monica woke in the morning, the last thing she wanted to do was peel herself away.

She wanted to be close to him, to have him near her at all times. At the same time, she felt this was a kind of gentle prison. She was a mother, a wife, a woman defined in relation to the men around her. But who did *she* want to be? Who was *she*?

Dr. Bellegarde suggested that the loss of Saundra was tied to a lingering sense of loss concerning her father, a professor of Religious Studies at Butler, who'd been diagnosed with terminal brain cancer when Monica was nine years old. The progress of the disease was steady, and treatment ultimately ineffective. There had been time to prepare—as much as a child that age can prepare to say good-bye to her father. At any rate, everyone knew what was coming. Remarkably, her father had kept his spirits up. He was thin and bald, he was trapped in a bed with a dozen tubes and patches and wires coming off him, but he would still wink when Monica came into his room, still pat her hand and say, "Hiya, Kiddo," just like he always had. For a long time, Monica had secretly believed that the doctors were wrong. It was some sort of horrendous mistake. The cancer would disappear, her father would miraculously improve, and this would all somehow go away.

Of course it didn't. Her father's condition gradually worsened, just as the doctors predicted. Those memories, so painful, were all blurred in Monica's mind. She had difficulty remembering just when things moved from bad to worse. Towards the end, her father was very ill and the doctor kept him loaded on morphine. He was unconscious for most of the final month, already sort of gone. When he'd died, Monica was told it was a blessing, the end of suffering, a release.

Part of her believed that. But as she'd moved into her adolescent and teen years, another, darker part, a secret part that she'd always kept inside, grew angry. Bitter. Resentful. The fact of the disease she understood; it was the other stuff, the *why* of it—the why him, why us, why now, why me—that she couldn't grasp. That's why she could laugh at the existential dilemmas of a sixteen-year-old: she'd been there. She'd had her arguments with God and the universe. She'd cursed the charlatans of modern medicine. And, for several years, she'd held a grudge against her mother and sister, for throughout the entire ordeal they had never given up hope. And so Monica had felt hopeful, too. But hope had proven to be a lie.

Monica handled the death poorly. Emotionally, she bounced back and forth like a pinball: angry at others one minute, reproaching herself the next. Her grades plummeted. Inquiries from the school principal, long sessions with the counselor, outright scoldings from her mother—nothing seemed to help. As if any of it would have made one damn bit of difference. You can't be rational when mourning a lost father. You don't think in linear progression. There's an initial period of craziness, gradually giving way to mere lunacy, followed by a quieter, but much more protracted madness. It is that world you eventually come to live in, if you are to survive. There is no going back.

Monday, Tuesday, Wednesday: all had been long days. But Thursday was shaping up to be the killer. Jacob had been cranky all morning, fussy and clingy and crying over any little thing. He was cutting a new tooth that was driving him nuts. And he was constipated. To top it off, he wouldn't go down for his afternoon nap. Wailing, crying, arms thrashing like a demented windmill, he stomped and jumped in his crib, pulling his dress up over his head and nearly choking himself. Monica was beside herself. She tried rocking him in her arms. She tried a warm bottle. She tried sitting out on the front porch. Jacob, red-faced and eyes tightly shut, kept crying.

Finally, as a kind of last resort, she forced him into his child seat in the car, making sure it was secure and tight. Then she climbed into the driver's seat of her Toyota and fastened her seatbelt. She popped a Dan Zanes CD into the stereo and took off north, driving deeper into Yolo Canyon. Houses there were farther and farther apart, and set back from the road. She turned off the paved two-lane road and onto a narrow, dirt road that wound up one side of the canyon. The road became a series of switchbacks, quite tricky and tight. Overgrown tree limbs hung low over the road like some lost woman's hair.

Within five minutes Jacob quit his crying and his breathing slowed. Fifteen minutes later, when she crested the canyon and pulled off onto a gravel turnout, he was down. She put the car in park and set the brake and, for fear of waking the baby, left the engine purring. Jacob was out cold, a delightful line of drool gracing his stumpy little chin. He looked so cute in his pink-and-blue dress! The hell with Jeff.

She got out of the car and stood there on the edge of the turnout, one foot lifted on to a rock, surveying the canyon below her. Now, in late spring, the hills were light green, the vibrant emerald grass of winter giving way, slowly, to the golden yellow of summer. The trees were thick with new leaves. There is something in a panorama that prompts meditation, driving us to larger questions. And the question forming in Monica's mind was why, with all this gorgeous territory spread before her, she had not fully entered into it, this place she now called home. She hadn't given her heart to it.

Her marriage, she had to admit, was in a kind of stasis. Jeff was buried in his work. Weekends home had become trying. About the time everyone was starting to relax and thaw out, it was time to pack a bag for the next week. "It's just temporary," he kept telling her. That, and it was going to pay off. What could she do but wait? Alone. She took the baby to the Saturday Farmer's Market alone. She took the baby to the playground alone. She took the baby to the grocery store, to the hardware store, to the shopping mall. Alone, alone, alone.

Not really alone. Jacob was the one thing, the one person to whom Monica gave herself without question or compromise—well, without dangerous, absurd or inconvenient compromise. In every other aspect of her life, she felt she dealt with everything through a kind of emotional shorthand. It was how she negotiated to avoid confrontation. It was how she rationalized her loneliness. And for as long as she'd understood this about herself, she'd pondered what to do about it. It sometimes seemed to her that she hadn't done anything about anything, except care for Jacob. A total occlusion of the self. Good stuff if you're a Buddhist. But she wasn't *only* a mother. She was also an aspiring writer. And this was 2006! In the twenty-first century, in a post-feminist era, those shouldn't be mutually exclusive categories. But it sure felt that way to Monica.

People said having kids made you alive, made you wake up and enjoy life. Bullshit! On any given day, she woke up feeling more or less grouchy, disoriented, and hungry. She fumbled around the kitchen like a spastic until she'd had a cup of really strong coffee. Her toddler mewled and gurgled as she spooned organic applesauce into his mouth, half of which ended up hanging from his chin like some overpriced spa salve. An hour or so later his diaper was full and she wrestled him down onto the changing table where she cooed into his face whilst wiping him clean. There were chores to be ignored or completed, depending on their urgency and her mood. There were meals to be cooked or microwaved, depending on whether she felt like being an artist or an automaton. Finally, at the end of the week, her husband appeared on the threshold, mysteriously tipping the chemistry in the house in unpredictable ways. Any normal woman would be glad to have what she had: a husband like Jeff, a son like Jacob, a home to call her own.

A tear rolled down Monica's cheek. She wiped it with her fingertips, then pressed its dampness deep into her palm. To absorb and accept: to draw in, not push out—in every way she sought to reverse the flow of love and energy in her life. The question was how, though she thought she was beginning to see a way out of it all.

She did not have to be who she was. That was the real hell of it: knowing that, and still finding yourself stuck, afraid to move. But she must not trick herself into thinking it would all change in an instant. She could reinvent herself, she knew that. But it would be gradual, slow—page-by-page, word-by-word. Like reading *David Copperfield*.

She got back into the car. The tears hadn't stopped, though she thought they would not come any faster. She had the strange desire to wake her son and apologize to him for something, though she wasn't sure just what. For not being who she wanted to be, if that made any sense. For having settled for less.

She accelerated down the hill, eyes wet, wiping away the tears. Her hands felt slightly slick on the steering wheel. She switched on the radio, punched in a classic rock station and immediately heard an old Fleetwood Mac song, "The Chain," one of her and Saundra's favorites. She recalled lying on her sister's bed, watching her cue up their mother's old copy of *Rumours* on the turntable. Together they studied the album art, the black-and-white insert. Monica was fascinated by the mysterious ballerina shot on the cover: Mick Fleetwood holds a crystal ball in his palm, mesmerizing Stevie Nicks. Saundra had memorized all the lyrics, sang softly along to every song. "The Chain" built slowly, from its sparse opening notes to the inevitable crescendo at the end, a loping bass line overlaid by a high, yearning guitar solo. Monica remembered prancing around her bedroom, plucking at strings of beads and necklaces, dancing like the gypsy Stevie Nicks. And then Saundra joining her, the girls holding hands and facing each other, fingers locked tight, singing the song's final lines in unison: *The chain keeps us together, running through the shadows....*

Monica reached for the car radio, fingers fumbling at the buttons in an attempt to turn it up. She took her eyes off the road, and it was at that moment something caught the corner of her eye, some movement to her right. A woman in a pale yellow dress stepping out of the forest and into the road.

Monica, driving a little too fast, jerked the steering wheel to the left. She felt the tires give way. Fishtailing, the car slid toward the side of the road until the rear end thumped with a hard jolt, her skull pounding against the head rest.

"Oh my god!" she blurted. She turned to check on Jacob in the back. For a long moment his chest was flat, still, unmoving.

Then came a big suck of air, one of those toddler gulps. His head wagged back and forth, gently. He never knew a thing.

She got out of the car, looking for this woman walking down the road. When Monica couldn't see her, she thought for a moment she'd hit the woman. But, no, she found no one. Monica quickly walked around her car. She got down on her knees and, muttering a quick prayer, looked under it. She scanned the hill above her. She called out. She heard only the rustling of tree limbs in the gentle afternoon breeze. She felt so certain that someone had been there. She felt it even then. A woman in a yellow dress.

It had to be a coincidence. Either that, or she was losing her mind.

A big white pickup truck came barreling down the road, a cloud of dust in its wake. The truck stopped in the middle of the road and a man in tight blue jeans and a Western shirt got out.

"Ma'am, are you all right?"

Monica nodded. "I lost control," she said. "Someone walked out of the woods. I nearly hit her. I swerved my car."

The man's eyes made a quick but thorough pass around the area. Then he turned his gaze on Monica. He walked over to examine her car.

"You checked on your daughter in there? She all right?"

"My son," Monica said. "Yes. He's fine."

The man turned a quizzical gaze on Monica. He walked around the back

32

of her car, then back up into the road. Her car was not stuck, he said, and she should be able to pull it back onto the road.

"Thank you," Monica said. "You didn't see anyone? A woman in a yellow dress?"

The man shook his head. There were no houses between here and the bottom of the canyon, he said. Few people walked this road, unless they were hunting. Most likely she saw a deer. They dart in and out of the woods quickly. Then he asked where she'd been headed. Monica said she lived nearby, on Yolo Canyon Road.

"I'll follow you down," the man said, "just to make sure you reach home safe."

Monica drove very slowly down the hill and back into the canyon, the white truck keeping a respectful distance in her rearview mirror. She parked in front of her house and waved in thanks to the man as he drove on. He tooted his horn in acknowledgment.

She sat quietly, listening to the engine tick. Her hands trembled. Her lips quivered. She was some kind of mess, she knew that.

Jacob woke with a large yawn. He stared, wide-eyed around him, then found his mother's eyes. He smiled, a big, full-lipped smile. "Mama," he said. "Mama."

Monica waited for the wave of joy, and finally it came, lifting her into its swirling current as she unstrapped him from his car seat and lifted him into the golden afternoon sunlight, her little prince in a dress, all golden curls and chubby cheeks. She held him tight, her one and only, her beloved, her Jacob.

4

Near the end of tenth grade, Monica received a letter from her high school inviting her to join Advanced Placement English. Her mother took this as a great compliment. Saundra had been invited to join AP English, Math, and Science, and was now on a scholarship at the University of Chicago. Though no one had said anything, Monica understood the same was expected from her. But what if you didn't want to be Miss Junior Achiever? What if you didn't care about yearbook, or team sports? Monica wasn't following anyone's footsteps. The age of hand-me-downs had ended when Monica had reduced her wardrobe to one color: black.

Monica let the deadline for responding to the invitation pass without comment. A second letter was followed by a phone call from her English teacher, who wanted to ask if the invitation had arrived. The school had heard no response.

When her mother asked about this, Monica bluntly announced that she didn't care to join any AP classes. The kids there were prigs and do-gooders. Over-achievers.

"It's a crucial step in building a strong application for college," her mother said. "The kind of thing recruiters look for."

Monica didn't care. She'd rather slug it out with the peons in regular English. That's where all her friends were, anyway.

"Your friends," her mother said, flatly.

Saundra, who happened to be home that weekend, had been listening in from the other side of the kitchen table. She looked up from her magazine.

"You're a fool, Monica. You only get this one chance. Don't blow it."

"And you're a twat," Monica snapped. "Go play with your slide rule."

"That's enough!" her mother shouted, and ordered Monica to her room.

"Exactly where I prefer to be," she quipped. She stormed down the hall, slamming her bedroom door shut.

Half an hour later, her sister rapped on her door. "Monica."

"Fuck off."

"Come out and see the television. Kurt Cobain is dead."

On the TV news, a reporter stood outside the gates of Cobain's house in Seattle, surrounded by hundreds of mourning fans. Cobain had taken his life with a gun. Monica threw herself into an armchair and listened as the reporter recounted what they knew of Cobain's final hours, which wasn't much. Monica sighed. Was it sad? Yes. Unexpected? Hardly. The band had just recorded a song called "I Hate Myself and I Want to Die." Cobain had posed for publicity pictures with a rifle in his mouth. In and out of rehab, he'd recently tried to overdose on pills after a show in Rome. It didn't take Sherlock Holmes to see it coming.

Like most teens her age, she'd been introduced to Nirvana's "Smells Like Teen Spirit" on MTV, where she'd watched the video countless times. She'd played the CD endlessly in her room. She liked everything about the record, from the big chunky power chords to the fumbling acoustic number. The lyrics were wry and derisive. The band didn't take itself too seriously. Witty, in a way. At any rate, she knew her mother would never understand, and that was all she needed to know.

She'd seen them once in Indianapolis at the Egyptian Ballroom. A rowdy, all-ages affair, with a teeming mosh pit of kids slamming into one another and clambering up on stage to take swan dives into the crowd, a shared melody of lust and sweat and pain. Monica's friends didn't want anything to do with it and hung back from the fray, clinging to their safe spots along the wall. After a half-dozen songs, she left them and waded into the hot press of bodies, where she was jostled and pushed, thumped and thrashed. A couple times she felt herself lifted off her feet, moved in one direction or another. Floating in the crowd, one of the masses.

On stage Cobain wore a brown trenchcoat. His shoulder-length blonde locks looked greasy and matted. A vacant, disinterested stare glossed his stubble-covered face, a look that said he didn't care if he were there or not. Monica couldn't believe that someone playing that kind of music—so loud, so fast, so heavy—could be so disengaged. Was he faking it? Going through the motions? Toward the end of the show the band started up a heavy, dirge-like song with a repetitious bass hook and pounding drums. Cobain stood back from his mic and let his hands fall from the guitar, which squealed and whined with distortion and white noise. He stood absolutely still as the rhythm section pounded along, locked in a groove. Then he turned and walked to the side of the stage. He knelt before his wall of amplifiers like a religious penitent or an errant child, asking for forgiveness. The caterwaul of electronic screeching continued, the variations in the feedback moving currents in an ocean of noise.

Hands clasping the cabinet walls, Cobain slowly, ritualistically pounded his skull against the speaker cabinets a dozen times. When he stood a minute later, he staggered. A line of blood ran down the side of his face, his eyes glazed in a fiery trance. He stepped to the microphone and released a primal roar, a thing of harrowing, nerve-scraping intensity, something directed somewhere very far away from that ballroom where a thousand kids slammed themselves into one another. Something in a language known only to him, a man lonely in a room filled with admirers, a man alive only through pain.

Monica received a letter from Indiana University reminding her that the five-year time limit on her master's program would shortly expire. Could she please inform them if she planned to re-enroll, to apply for an extension, or to withdraw? Monica left the letter on the kitchen table for a couple of days, unsure what to do about it. She'd made it halfway through the program, so she still had quite a lot of coursework to finish, including her thesis. She made some phone calls. Completing the degree via correspondence wasn't an option. The adviser at Indiana suggested she look into transferring to a California school. So she telephoned the English Department at Chico State and spoke to the graduate director. Yes, she could transfer a certain amount of course work from Indiana. It'd be nigh on starting over, but if she took a couple of classes a term she could finish in two years. And it was fairly cheap. They talked over the specifics of the application: entrance exams, a statement of purpose, and letters of recommendation. And she'd need a writing sample. The professor asked what genre she was writing in.

"Creative nonfiction."

"Then we'll need an essay or two," he said. "Your very best stuff."

When she got off the phone, she couldn't sit down. She paced in a circle around the living room. She had a deadline: August first. She would need to have one or two essays ready to submit on August first.

But with Jeff gone all week, how was she going to be able to write? She could only do so much on the weekends. Weekday mornings were the only time she could carve out. Slipping quietly out of bed at six, she had at least an hour or two before Jacob woke. Sometimes this worked, sometimes it didn't. It was very inconsistent.

One morning, she sat down at the laptop and began to read over the new essay she was working on. She'd just gotten twenty minutes into it—she was still brushing the cobwebs out of her mind, waiting for the caffeine to kick in—when Jacob's first, plangent wail broke the stillness.

"Mommy!"

That was it, she knew, until nap time. (If she didn't want to clean the kitchen or balance the checkbook.) Or maybe after bed-time. (If she didn't want to do laundry, watch television, or collapse in a heap.) She was a writer, or wanted to be a writer, but had no writing time. She was a full-time, stay-at-home mother of a toddler living in rural Butte County, California, surrounded by dope farmers, political conservatives, and evangelical Christians. She lived miles from the nearest coffee shop, art gallery, or decent bookstore, and had been all but abandoned by her commuter husband. Oh, and she was about to have a nervous breakdown. That's who she was.

Monica went to Jacob. He stood at the rail of the crib, arms outstretched, his desire for her naked, clear, irrefusable. His round apple cheeks were rosy red. On the bedding, a circle of drool. Joy washed over Monica, like a powerful wave surging onto a beach. Singing a little song, she changed his diaper, then took him into bed with her where they cuddled for thirty minutes.

Jeff said she coddled him. When Monica complained about being a de facto single parent, he started talking about daycare. Give the kid a taste of social interaction, he said. Give Monica some time to herself. She'd thought about it. She had several girlfriends with kids in daycare, at least part-time. But she could never bring herself to act. It didn't feel right. Jeff told her to get over it. Once she "liberated herself" she'd wonder why it took her so long. But what did he know? He hadn't carried a baby around for nine months, hadn't nursed it and cuddled it and held it, knowing that a miracle had occurred: out of her body had come this magical person, so awake and aware and alive. So totally dependent and vulnerable. When he cried, her gut tightened. When he was happy, her heart sang.

In two years, Monica had never been away from Jacob for more than a few hours. She'd been there every morning when he woke. He could never go to daycare! She'd home-school him! Make him work from home! She'd cook dinner for him every night! He would never leave her!

After breakfast, she plunked Jacob in front of the television and thereby bought herself some forty minutes to write, but she felt guilty the whole time. She was convinced that television would rot his brain. (Thomas the Tank Engine, invented by an Anglican priest and designed to teach the British proletariat to accept cheerfully their place in the social order.) Plus it's a lousy excuse for a babysitter. She got exactly no writing done because she needed to be within eyesight of the little guy, which, combined with the noise of the show, and Ringo Starr being its narrator, distracted the hell out of her.

Okay, screw the fairytale. The kid is going to daycare.

As a means to buy time, of course, for her writing and reading. Because she was serious about graduate school, serious about her writing, serious about nurturing that part of her life.

Monica spent the better part of the next week visiting local daycares. She was surprised to find one provider just ten minutes away, in a small town. She visited the place, a tiny, in-home operation—one harried mother and her two kids, plus a half-dozen preschoolers. And chickens in the yard. And dogs chasing the chickens. And a white truck in the driveway with mud-spattered side panels.

Into Chico she went. She visited church daycares, and big operations in stand-alone buildings with shiny, institutional floors. There were daycares with art and music programs, daycares with field trips, and Spanish-immersion daycares. She settled on one that looked like a little red barn and had a platoon of cheerful, young women (they were always cheerful, young women) in matching golf shirts who guaranteed a lower teacher-to-student ratio than the other places. One afternoon nap period a day, plus snacks. Monica would pack a lunch.

She and Jeff discussed it on the phone.

"Do it," he said. "Take back your life."

"Don't say it like that," she replied. "Jacob doesn't take anything from me."

"Except all your time. Anyway, it'll be good for him. A little taste of the big world. He's ready for it, believe me. But, Monica, please, no dresses at daycare."

Initially, Monica arranged to leave Jacob just two days a week. On the first day, she dutifully packed his lunch and got him dressed in a cute T-shirt and blue jeans, and they drove into Chico to the daycare. Monica brought him in to his room and introduced him to his teachers and his fellow students. She played with him for a few minutes to help ease the transition, then sat in a little toddler chair in the corner of the room, watching as he played with the other kids.

Thirty minutes later, one of the teachers approached.

"He's doing fine," she said. "You could sneak out."

But Monica felt it would be cruel. Jacob kept glancing over his shoulder, looking for his mother. Every time he saw her, he smiled and returned to playing with his blocks or toy cars. What would he do when he looked for her and she was gone? She felt certain the experience would scar him. So she stayed. Her back ached from sitting in the undersized chair. At noon, she gave into her inner Mom and checked Jacob out.

"I think we've had enough for the first day," she said.

The daycare teachers smiled with understanding. That's okay, they said, it didn't hurt to do things gradually.

Two days later, Monica arrived at the daycare resolved to leave promptly, like the other parents she'd observed: drop, kiss, and run. She put Jacob down, stayed with him for a few minutes until he'd become absorbed in arranging felt shapes on a table, and then leaned over and kissed him and said, "Good-bye."

"Good-bye," Jacob repeated.

Monica stood and smoothed her trousers. Maybe she'd get lucky, she thought, and he would accept her departure. She took a deep breath, turned, and quietly made her way for the door. Trembling, her fingers fumbled as she unfastened the half-door separating her from the toddler corral and the larger daycare, a succession of rooms without walls.

"Mommy stay, Mommy stay!"

She turned. Jacob ran to her, burying his face in her trousers, and exploded into tears. Monica's willpower all but collapsed.

After a minute, one of the teachers came over and gave her a knowing nod. Though every instinct told her to grab Jacob and flee, she returned the nod. The teacher knelt down and slowly, gently peeled Jacob off his mother. Jacob's little arms flew about like angry snakes. He stomped his feet, screaming. The teacher restrained him with a bear hug, mouthing, "Go!"

Monica double-timed it for the exit, her son's shrill cries echoing in the hallway, blackening her fickle heart.

She held it together until she got into her car. Then she let herself go, sobbing into a tissue. She was a terrible mother! If this was what she needed to do to "reclaim her life"—to inflict pain and suffering on her son—she was more than willing to give it up.

When she calmed down, she drove two blocks down the street to a coffee shop and sat there with a café au lait and a newspaper, though she could only read half-heartedly. Was Jacob bawling now? It felt strange not knowing. A knot of anxiety tightened in her stomach. She'd left her son with total strangers! She buried her face in her hands. What was she doing?

She resisted the urge to call the center on her cell phone, or to drive down the block and peek in. Eventually, she drove herself home, where she booted up the laptop and sat down with—good God!—a whole day to write. And she did write for an hour or so, but not well. All the while she felt distracted, nervous. Out of sorts. She spent the rest of the day cleaning the house.

When she picked up Jacob at four, he was fine. Happily playing by himself in a corner with a fire truck. She asked the teachers how he'd done, bracing herself for a litany of horrors.

"He had a great day. He quit crying ten minutes after you left. They're all like that at first."

Monica couldn't believe it. She thanked the teachers, gave Jacob the biggest hug of all time, and then drove him home, where she fed him a quick snack and put on a Madonna record. She kicked off her shoes, spun in a quick circle, and held her hands out, inviting her toddler to join her. She held his hands as he stood, a bit wobbly on his legs, and stamped his feet as they danced to "Lucky Star." Jacob giggled and smiled with toddler glee. Monica threw her head back and laughed. This was how to be happy.

5

After her junior year at Purdue, Monica decided to take some time off. She was not technically dropping out, as her mother bewailed. She just needed time to breathe, time to step away and reconsider. Her heart wasn't in her school work, and her grades showed it.

Monica rented a room in a big Victorian house in Broad Ripple, Indianapolis, a neighborhood filled with artists, left-leaning political activists, and assorted wayward travelers. She took a job waiting tables at a café/art gallery and decided she'd learn to play bass guitar. She auditioned for several bands before finally finding Model Farm, a cow-punk outfit fronted by a wiry, thin guy with tattoos up and down his arms. He wore oversized glasses and Western shirts, scuffed cowboy boots, and played a Fender Telecaster covered in Hüsker Dü and Black Flag stickers. His name was Clinton. He was from Muncie and, as he put it, he was never fucking going back. Clinton wrote weird, funny songs about the lives of insects, picnics on the moon, and women who thought God was on the telephone. Watching him for just half an hour, Monica understood he had a strange charisma, some charm on stage that was rare. When he sang his songs, his skinny limbs flailing around, thrashing on his Telecaster like a maniac, there was something utterly compelling about him, like David Byrne gone to seed.

Monica loved him, for a time. He was difficult to talk to, quarrelsome when drunk, and impossibly moody when sober. She liked him best when he was writing songs, for then he had a playful, boyish joy about him. He loved to share a new tune, belting it out on a battered acoustic in her kitchenette. Here was a man who, when he needed an audience, made love to it. The problem was he didn't need that audience often enough.

Six months into their relationship, Monica missed her period. She gave it a few days, a week. And though she was nervous, she said nothing to Clinton, afraid of his response. After ten days, however, she was beside herself, and she blurted it out. Clinton's response was immediate and practical: they had to get a home pregnancy test. Now. They did, and the result was negative. Two days later, Monica got her period.

Not long after that, Monica sat at the small table in her cramped kitchenette while Clinton chopped vegetables for a late-morning omelet. The smell of sautéing onions and garlic filled the room. Monica idly flipped through a day-old copy of the *Indianapolis Star*.

"Just curious," she said, "what would you have done if that test had been positive?"

"What test?"

"The pregnancy test."

"I wouldn't have done anything," he said, dropping a handful of chopped tomato into the skillet. "You would've gotten an abortion."

Monica looked up from the editorial page. "How do you know that?"

"Because I'm never going to have a fucking kid. I'm never getting married, never getting chained to a mortgage or a car payment or a person. I don't want to own the earth. I don't want to owe anybody anything. I reject all that phony, middle-class bullshit."

He rapped the cutting board with the flat of the knife. Then he gestured with a thumb towards the stovetop. "Can I put hot peppers in this omelet?"

Monica looked at this man, with his acne-scarred face and triple-pierced ears, the tongue of a tattoo jutting up from the neckline of his T-shirt, and she felt like crying.

"You're asking my permission to put hot peppers in an omelet," she said.

He gave her a look. "Yeah. A simple yes or no."

"I'm not hungry," she said, and left the room.

Two months later Clinton announced that he'd be taking the band to Los Angeles. Was she in? Just like that—so blunt, so black-and-white. Monica said she'd already enrolled for fall classes. She was going to give college another try. It was a lie, but it allowed her leave on her terms and not give Clinton the satisfaction of dropping her. He left with a muted good-bye, he and his faithful drummer driving west in that shitty van. Monica never heard from him again. Disappeared, she'd assumed, into the sinkhole that is L.A.

Shortly before that, the band played a show in Chicago. Monica thought she might phone her sister. They hadn't spoken in a while. Monica wasn't particularly good about returning phone calls, having fallen into yet another icy détente with her mother and her minions (i.e., Saundra) since dropping out of college. Plus, Saundra was beyond busy. But, after Monica left a couple of messages, Saundra did call her back, and they quickly caught up. That winter Saundra was in her final year of law school at Northwestern. Her life was books, case studies, court briefings. And a boyfriend, Mark, who'd been a year ahead of her and was now clerking for a firm in Aurora, out in the 'burbs. An hour commute each way. With Saundra's long hours in the law library and Mark's willingness to work fourteen hour days for his uncle, they hardly saw each other.

Monica said she knew it was a long shot on a Tuesday night, but her band would be at the Cubby Bear, across the street from Wrigley Field. They were the first band on a three-band bill, with a forty-five-minute slot. Seven-dollar cover charge.

Saundra said she'd see what she could do, and wished her good luck regardless.

Model Farm hit the stage at ten. The bar was nearly empty, the mood dull and the band tired. She and Clinton had quarreled earlier and weren't speaking. Twenty minutes into their set, Saundra showed up, alone. She was dressed like a lawyer, in her smart pants suit and coiffed hair. Totally out of place. But she sat at a table in the back and nursed a drink. After the show Monica all but ran to her.

"I didn't think you'd make it."

"I almost didn't." She rubbed her brow. She talked about her workload, how the partners in the firm just kept piling it on. "You can't say no to anything. It's the worst kind of exploitation, something out of a Dickens novel."

"It'll pay off when you're making six figures."

"If they don't work me to death first."

Monica asked about Saundra's boyfriend. Wrong question. Saundra's face screwed up in pain. "We broke up."

"Oh, shit. Sorry. I wouldn't have mentioned it if I'd known."

Saundra shook her head. "He's got a sweet position out in Aurora. He wanted to move out there so he can put in his seventy hours. I said no way. There's other things," she said, waving a hand diffidently. "They're grooming him. He's extremely smart. And ambitious. He tries to be kind, but...."

"You don't look so good," Monica said.

Saundra sank her face into her hands. "I feel like shit. I can't sleep."

On stage, Clinton and the drummer were breaking down their equipment, even as the next band was setting theirs up. Monica decided against mentioning her boyfriend to Saundra. If introduced, Clinton could be icy, or worse. It occurred to her, not for the first time, that they wouldn't be together much longer.

"Look, I have to pack up my gear. Can you stick around for a half-hour or so?"

Saundra looked at her watch. She had to be in the office the next morning by seven. At this rate, she'd be lucky to get five hours' sleep.

"I'm glad you made it," Monica said. "Really, I am."

Saundra rubbed her brow. "I'm going to pay for it tomorrow, I can tell you."

Monica said that next time they were in Chicago she'd try to give her more lead-time. They could get together for lunch or dinner, they'd have time to talk. Next time.

The circles under Saundra's eyes were dark and puffy. "That'd be nice," she said.

They hugged, pecked each other on the cheek. And then Saundra was gone.

6

With some of the essays, Monica could invent. Extrapolate. Enter into her sister's experience or one very similar to it and flesh out all the details. She wrote an essay about Saundra losing her virginity. Monica knew the who and the when, and vaguely where, but little more. So she simply drew from her own experience of wrestling with a half-drunk high school sophomore (Tommy Golando, bless you, you're forgiven) on the shag carpet of the boy's living room at the absurd hour of three-thirty in the afternoon, rushing the deed to prevent being caught by the boy's mother, due home from work within the hour. Monica was sure her sister's experience mirrored her own in every important way: the comical inexperience of the lovers fumbling at each other's waistbands; the heady rush of fear and desire; the boy's hasty, selfish orgasm; the nearly total absence of sexual enjoyment for Saundra.

The essay, like the boyfriend, came quickly. Just over ten pages, it was a compact sketch with a clean dramatic arc that Monica figured would be revised, expanded, or framed by some other narrative. She printed a hard copy and set it aside. A few days later, when she thought she could be objective, she took it onto the back porch to read it, pencil in hand. Ordinarily, she did not spare herself, slashing lines, re-arranging paragraphs, scribbling new sentences in the margins. This time, she read the essay through without making a single mark. At first, she thought she'd not read carefully or critically enough. So she re-read it. Again, no edits.

She chewed her lower lip. This was good, she thought. It might be very good. She might mail this one out, just to see if an editor would take it.

She lifted her eyes from the page, tapped the yellow pencil on the corner of the manuscript. Below her, the burbling waters of Yolo Creek murmured its soft song, the water rolling along merrily. A scrub jay squawked from the branch of a nearby sycamore, its call piercing and shrill.

From inside the house came a clatter and bang: the sound of a cooking pot being knocked or rattled. Loud and distinct. The sound startled and disturbed her, a sudden prick of fear. She stood and walked into the house, manuscript in hand. In the kitchen, a sauce pot had fallen from the drying rack to the floor, the lid a few feet away. She was one to pile dishes on the drying rack in a perilous mountain, but since Monica was basically cooking dinner for one these days, there were rarely many dishes to clean, and the drying rack was just half-full. She didn't remember stacking the pot haphazardly. She bent and picked up the sauce pot from the floor.

When she heard the creak of floorboards, the press of a soft step, Monica froze in the middle of the kitchen floor, pot in one hand, manuscript in the other.

"I hear you," she said, loudly. "Why don't you just tell me what you want?"

She hesitated for a moment, listening.

"I'm not coming back there. You come out here. Show yourself."

After a minute, when she'd heard nothing more, she moved to the kitchen sink. As she gave the pot and lid a quick wash, she looked out the kitchen window at the back yard. One squirrel chased another around the trunk of a fat oak, the two of them corkscrewing their way up into the tree. Monica put the clean pot and lid in the drying rack.

Drying her hands on a towel, she told herself to forget about all this. Their house was old and noisy, it might have been anything—mice, or a pine cone dropping onto the roof. Who knew what. Or, okay, maybe it was a ghost, and so what if it was? Ghosts were just another tenant—not a rent-paying contributor to the domestic economy, but still. Another being to be tolerated and endured. Perhaps that was all this ghost wanted, after all. A little recognition. Or an offering.

Her sessions with Dr. Bellegarde had become occasional. She missed an appointment one week, and then he had to cancel a couple of weeks later. At her last visit, two weeks prior, she'd left a couple of essays with him, just to show him how things were progressing. She came to her next session, she had to admit, more than a little excited to hear his opinion of the work. But he didn't mention it. Instead, he wanted her to talk about latent feelings of aggression toward her mother. Wasn't it possible that she, Monica, was projecting or displacing her own anger onto Claudia?

"You mean am I being unfair to my mother."

He sat with his elbows up on the armrests of his large office chair, hands clasped over his belly, the tips of his two index fingers tapping out some kind of Morse code.

"Are you?"

"Is that a crime?"

Bellegarde smiled. "Of course not. Like I've said, it's quite common.

The salient question would be whether doing so prevents you from enacting closure and moving forward with your life."

"I love it when you talk shop to me. Say that again."

Bellegarde lifted his eyebrows and sat forward. "You're not exactly engaging me in this conversation today. You don't seem committed to this process. Why is that?"

"I want to know what you think about my writing."

"Ah, your essays."

Bellegarde opened one of the manila folders on his desk and took out the manuscripts. They looked pristine and white. Monica looked for a bent corner, a fold near the staple, a penciled comment—any evidence that he'd read them.

The writing is very good, he said. Excellent, in fact. But as he read, he had to keep in mind that the written word is a construction, a fabrication. It was a little like interpreting a dream: one had to be careful about making direct correlations between what was on the page and what the patient may have experienced. For instance, he was puzzled by the fact that she'd adopted her sister's name in the essay.

"Why wouldn't I?" Monica said. "It's about her."

Bellegarde furrowed his bushy brow. "But the essay is written in the first person."

"I'm writing her autobiography."

"You mean her biography."

"No. It's not me talking about her. I *am* her. On the page, in her voice. Sort of."

Bellegarde sat back in his chair, resuming the finger tapping. He asked if all the chapters in the autobiography were in the first-person. Monica said that they were. Was she working from some sort of rough draft, or notes? Were there journals she was transcribing?

"No," Monica said. "It's all from memory."

"Yet, in this essay," he said, "you get inside the mind of a sixteen-year-old girl on the day she loses her virginity. Her first-person thoughts, memories, desires—it's all on the page. If this is nonfiction, if this is your sister's biography, where did that come from?"

"It's speculation," Monica said. "Like you said, I'm filling in the blanks."

Bellegarde nodded slowly. "Don't you think 'fiction' would be a more accurate label?"

Monica shrugged her shoulders. "But it's not exactly fiction. It's what happened, sort of."

Bellegarde quarreled with her on this point. He saw no reason why she couldn't assume the viewpoint of any given character on the page. But to call such her exercise nonfiction seemed dubious. The reader would naturally assume that the first-person memoir voice was her own. If it was not, if she was writing in the voice of another, some kind of ghost writing or what-have-you, and if she didn't have evidence of one sort or another—if she freely admitted she'd filled in the blanks with fabricated thoughts, details, and so forth—then he supposed she must call it fiction.

"But you of all people know the vicissitudes of memory," Monica countered. "I'm thinking artistic license here. I'm thinking James Frey."

Bellegarde sat quietly for a moment, then cleared his throat. Yes, he said, the lines were often fuzzy, and memory is fluid. But if you take the kind of license Frey took, inventing episodes that didn't occur, claiming things happened to you that never did, then that was a fundamental violation of the unspoken agreement between the reader of a memoir and its author: that what is written down really happened, and that the memoirist has made a good faith effort to record it with both accuracy and honesty.

"Would you lie to me, to your therapist? Would you tell me you did things, or that people did things to you, that had never occurred? We have an agreement, you and I. You're going to tell me the truth, or at least be as truthful as you can possibly be. A memoirist operates by the same principle."

Monica knew he was right, in a sense. But she also knew that she didn't think of it that way. There were other kinds of truths. Truths that you could only arrive at through a back door, by erecting a façade of one sort or another. Because to approach some things head-on, taking dead aim at the bull's eye, was a kind of paralysis, or death. But she couldn't explain that to him, or perhaps to anyone. It didn't make sense in the way that they expected. She wasn't sure it made sense to her, except that she felt, deep down inside, in that mysterious, inky black part of her soul, that she must wear a kind of mask if she were to deliver the lines she needed to recite, to say the things that must be said. She was an actress working off-stage, playing her role out in the street.

But that wasn't her true mistake, finally. Her true mistake was in expecting people not to react, not to complain, to simply accept her choices. In order to progress on this project, in order to create this role, she had to stop asking people to take it straight. And that meant finding another angle of approach.

At her request, Bellegarde returned her manuscripts. He asked about scheduling the next month of visits. Monica asked to hold off. She needed to think.

"I've upset you," he said. "I've insulted your work."

"No," she said. "Honestly, this has been good. I need to hear what people are going to say. Because I do want to this work to find an audience."

"As fiction."

"I don't know," she said, simply. "I don't know how to explain it yet."

Bellegarde slowly stroked his beard. "Perhaps you don't have to explain it yet. I can see you're engaged by this process. Perhaps the best thing is to keep writing."

Yes, said Monica. On that point they could agree. She began gathering her things, making ready to leave.

"Do you believe in ghosts?" she asked him.

"No."

"You treat people with delusions."

"Occasionally."

"Ever treat somebody who thinks she sees people who aren't there?"

"I'm not sure what you're getting at."

"Ghosts. Everybody knows they're not real, but what if you think you've seen one? Isn't that serious?"

"It might be." Bellegarde sat forward in his chair. "But you're not… Monica, are you seeing people? Or hearing voices?"

"No voices," she said quickly. "I'm not *that* crazy, thank God. It's just that, once or twice now…."

Bellegarde raised his eyebrows, fingertips touching before him like a fan.

"There's no way for me to say this without sounding like an idiot."

"So just blurt it out, unedited. There's no judgment here."

Monica chewed her lower lip. "I think I'm haunted."

Bellegarde's eyes narrowed, just slightly. "You? Not your house?"

Monica explained that she'd heard things, the footsteps, and seen the sliver of a figure moving away from her in her house. And then the woman on the road, stepping in front of her car.

"I don't even believe in ghosts. I'm the biggest skeptic there is when it comes to this stuff." She rubbed a finger over her knuckles, red and chapped. "That's why I can't figure it. Who it is. Why. Why me. All of that."

Bellegarde ran a thumb along the lapel of his coat. He asked if she was very serious about this. If she truly believed she was seeing something—a ghost and not just a trick of the light, or some such.

"I'm not sure," Monica said, softly. "Probably I shouldn't have mentioned it."

"It certainly opens a new chapter," Bellegarde said. But they'd already run over their time for that week. He said he'd like to discuss the topic, first thing, at their next meeting.

Monica collected her things and stood from her chair.

"Thanks," she said, on her way out the office door. "Thanks for everything."

"Monica," the doctor said.

"I'll call you," she said, smiling, though of course this was a lie.

Leaving Bellegarde, Monica walked into the heart of downtown Chico. It was a cool spring afternoon. Earlier, there had been a spatter of rain. Dark, billowy clouds scudded by on swift inland breeze, all the moist, cool air blowing up the North Sacramento Valley from the Bay area. In City Plaza a group of teens skateboarded in one corner. She sat on a bench near the chess tables. Homeless guys played each other there, the ground littered with plastic coffee lids, beer caps, and half-smoked cigarettes. She watched someone else's toddler stomp after a pigeon, like a demented Godzilla. So much pleasure in this life comes at the expense of others.

Across the plaza stood an independent bookstore, the only one in town. Monica supported the idea of an independent bookstore in Chico. She made it a point to buy books there regularly, though she hadn't bought one recently. She stood from the bench, crossed the plaza and walked into the small, homey bookshop. The clerk greeted her with a bright, "Hello!" Monica browsed the fiction section for a good while, reading dust jacket blurbs. She picked up the latest hardcover from Joyce Carol Oates, something about a girl gang and the terrible things teens do. She opened the book to the first chapter and read the first page as she stood in the aisle. The writing was crisp, assured. A healthy dose of menace right there on page one. Monica walked to the front of the store. The clerk was not there. Monica heard her talking with a customer an aisle away.

She waited, staring out the shop window onto the street. A tall, thin woman in a yellow dress approached the store window. Her arms were folded across her midriff, one hand wrapped around a wrist. Her long, brown hair had been pulled back tightly against her head and fasted in a tight bun at the base of her neck. She had high cheekbones, and a narrow, angular face. Very pale. She stood for a long moment, gazing intently at the window display, then lifted her eyes and fixed them dead on Monica. The eyes were a haunting, pale gray—the color of overcast skies, as if the clouds had found their way inside. As Monica held the woman's gaze, she felt an odd sensation of recognition. A memory from early childhood washed over her.

She stands on a bridge overlooking a muddy river. Boughs of sycamore and oak hang low over the banks, spattered with buds and new leaves. Her hand rests on the cold railing of the bridge, and another, larger hand covers it, warming it. Her father.... A battered, aluminum-hulled bass boat shoots out from under the bridge, its outboard motor thrumming rhythmically. The boat's wide white wake spreads like a zipper opening, waves reaching for opposite shores. The ripples gradually subside, fading back into the brown water.

Monica turned abruptly, colliding with a shop clerk, who uttered a sharp cry as she spilled an armload of stationary.

Blurting an apology, Monica dropped the Oates novel into her shoulder bag. She stepped forward, intent on helping the clerk, who was fussily trying to collect the scattered stationary.

She looked up. The woman in the yellow dress had gone.

Monica bristled with adrenaline, a thin film of perspiration on her brow. That woman's gaze had somehow reached inside her, stirring something. The hand of an old soul. Monica had to see her again, see those eyes. She darted out the front door. The sidewalk was empty. She took a few hurried steps to peer down an alleyway—empty. The only possible place the woman could have gone would be the post office, though it was half a block away and she couldn't have made it up the steps and inside in such a short time. Monica hurried down the street and galloped up the steps. There was a sizeable queue in the lobby, people clutching boxes and padded envelopes, but no woman in a yellow dress.

Monica walked outside. From the top of the post office steps she surveyed City Plaza. People sat on the benches, or lay on the grassy knolls. Children raced through the jets of water as parents sat a safe distance away, nursing tall coffees in paper cups. But she saw no sign of the woman she sought. That woman was gone.

Driving home, with Jacob strapped safely into the back seat of her Toyota, Monica tried to convince herself that she hadn't exactly stolen an expensive new hardcover from her favorite, struggling independent bookstore. In the haste and anxiety of that moment, hadn't she just sort of unconsciously dropped the book in her bag? Wasn't it an instinctive, unthinking response? Collateral damage? Heat of the moment?

Not exactly, dearie.

In her heart of hearts, she had to admit that at least some part of her had been aware of her action. She'd known that, if dropping the book momentarily in the bag wasn't exactly wrong, darting out the door with it constituted a crime. She was a criminal. A petty criminal, but a criminal nevertheless, and the burden of even the smallest crime weighs heavy on an honest heart. Or it should. And so Monica felt remorse, or tried to. She knew she ought to feel it more than she did.

Hell, she wasn't going to force it. The fact of her crime was a neat and tidy item she could trot out as evidence, if need arose.

And, of course, if she really wanted to be on the square, she could stop by the store and pay for the damn thing. She would explain what'd happened, they'd all have a good laugh, and everything would be set straight.

They'd think she was crazy. Hearing footsteps in your house was one thing. But driving your car into a ditch because you thought you were going to hit someone who wasn't there, or stealing a book because you were running out into the street to catch a glimpse of someone who wasn't there (or was she?)—those were in a different category of behavior. Delusional, perhaps. Dangerous.

A cold spike of fear shot down Monica's neck, tingling her shoulders and arms. She didn't know if she could trust herself.

Honestly. What if it continued? What if it got worse?

Because here was the weird part: in each instance, on that country road and on that city street, she'd seen someone. She felt as certain of that as she felt about anything. And those eyes, those gray eyes, eyes the color of an ocean rain—she couldn't forget those eyes.

Of course, it made no sense. It defied logic and reason.

At home, she tried to clear her mind of this nonsense. She changed Jacob's diaper, fed him two heaping bowls of macaroni and cheese, poured him three cups of milk (didn't they feed the kid at daycare?), and then let him loose. Sated and full, he sat down like a fireplug in the middle of the living room floor and commenced to thumping with his own beloved malfeasance, Henry the Hammer.

7

Monica and Jacob slept in late the next morning, an indulgence that had, with Jeff's ongoing absences during the weekdays, become standard. It was not uncommon for them to linger in bed, snuggling and cuddling. That morning, a Friday, Monica was awakened by the telephone. Groggy from oversleeping, she fumbled for the phone and blurted out a thick, "Hello?" It was her mother calling from her office at Butler. She'd just finished her seminar on metaphysics and was grabbing a bite of lunch before office hours. She was pondering how best to use her spring break, she said. And it had occurred to her that, rather than grade student papers and catch up on reading, she'd like to come and visit her grandson in California. What did Monica think?

Monica, still wiping the proverbial cobwebs from her mind, sat up in bed. She realized an answer was customary after a question had been asked.

"Uh, great. Like, for the whole week?"

"Well, four or five days, at least. It's a long flight out there. And you don't seem keen on coming to Indiana."

Claudia had visited California just once, when Jacob was six months old. Claudia had insisted on staying in town at a hotel. "I know the life of a newborn," she'd said. "Crying in the middle of the night, diaper changes, and rocking chairs. You need your space, I need my sleep." The matriarch would not be swayed. Monica or Jeff had to drive into town each day to pick her up, and then drive her back at night. Two hours in the car, just getting to and fro. The visit had been brief, a mere three days, one morning of which Claudia had spent visiting an old friend in the philosophy department at the university.

And so, on that Friday morning, Monica made a point of gently insisting that Claudia stay at the house in Yolo Canyon. Jeff was out of town for five days a week, every week, she reminded her mother. She meant to suggest she'd appreciate the adult company (even if it was with her mother; she'd take what she could get), but Claudia heard it differently.

"I understand, dear. You want your mother at the house. You need the help."

Oh, just the way she said that! So patronizing, so condescending! Like

Monica couldn't manage. Claudia was always doing that: turning things around on you, making it seem like she was the savior and you, you were helpless, incompetent. It was an old trick, one that Saundra had pointed out to Monica years ago.

Saundra, then a graduate student at Northwestern, had driven down to West Lafayette to check on her little sister. One night, they sat in a booth at the Knickerbocker, a favorite watering hole, nursing a second round of cocktails. In her probing, lawyer-like way, Saundra was asking why Monica and Claudia weren't speaking to one another. Their relationship had become a Cold War détente, with Saundra as the go-between for nearly everything.

"Mom won't talk about it. She says to ask you. So, what's up?"

Monica described the most recent berating-via-telephone from Claudia, who only seemed only to find fault in her youngest child. Monica had gotten a "C" in Astronomy. (Actually, not a bad grade in that class, a famous weed-out course designed to cull the majors from the daytrippers). Monica was a second-semester sophomore, yet to declare a major. (Actually, she was contemplating a self-designed B.A. and had met three times with an adviser that semester.) Monica wasn't socially active. She hadn't pledged a sorority. (They were all self-righteous bitches.) She hadn't joined any campus organizations. (Ditto.) The only noteworthy thing she'd done was to play the ghost of Miss Jessel in an adaptation of *The Turn of the Screw*, which, surprisingly, Claudia had driven down to see on back-to-back nights. (A production panned by the campus drama critic, a snotty senior with a stick up his ass. Claudia had written a lengthy letter to the editor of the student newspaper, quoting Aristotle and Ibsen, much to the amusement of Monica, her fellow thespians, and the professor who directed the play.) Claudia had fired all of this at Monica both barrels, in a tyrannical monologue rivaling any blowhard out of Shakespeare. (Sit down, Polonius.) Monica couldn't get a word in edgewise, so she'd finally taken the brash step of hanging up on her mother. That'd been nearly a month ago.

"I can't talk to her," Monica told Saundra. "Literally. I cannot speak one word. I'm supposed to listen to her attack me and thank her afterwards. She dominates and bullies the conversation. Then she wonders why I resent her. I'll tell you what she is: she's blind. And deaf, at least when I want to talk."

Saundra sat back in her chair, sipping her drink. Then she leaned forward and told Monica that, yes, their mother was always assuming a position of authority, always seeking to define the terms of an engagement before the other person could, and thereby hold an advantage.

"She's a master of rhetoric," Saundra concluded.

"Great! Only this isn't a lecture hall. This is a family, or it's supposed to be. I'm her daughter, not her student."

Saundra nodded. "I hear you. But let me tell you one thing I've learned in law school. I'm up against some of the same things Mom has had to deal with. She's a smart, professional woman in a career dominated by stuffy old men. And in philosophy, to boot, which is *nothing* but stuffy old men. And she's a single mother. She can't sit back and be a wallflower. She has to strike the first blow, so to speak. She's tough that way. I respect her."

That explanation only deepened Monica's unease. It made her feel guilty and unappreciative. Shouldn't she be proud of her mother, too?

No! Her mother was a tyrant and a bitch!

In the years that followed, that conversation had come to signify a crucial difference between Monica and her older sister. Secretly, Monica had always harbored a grudge against Saundra, who was so plainly out to follow in their oh-so-distinguished mother's footsteps. Saundra had always been Miss Junior Overachiever, Miss Do The Family Proud. Was it petty to reject that? Not necessarily. The question would be the quality of the alternative, and that's where Monica always tripped herself up, for she was the first to admit that her plans erred on the side of simplicity: to loiter, linger and languish in college not only because, true enough, choosing a major seemed like a daunting thing (*You want to be a tax accountant?* she said to one boyfriend. *At nineteen, you know that?*), but also because, well, let's just call a spade a spade: to be a procrastinator, an under-achiever, to be an artist was to be the exact opposite of her mother. Assertion in the form of rebellion. Definition by means of opposition. Yes, it was a protracted adolescence. Monica could admit as much. But she'd outgrown it. No, really, she had!

Jeff arrived home late that night. He stepped in the door, one shoulder bent under the weight of his black laptop bag. His shirt was untucked. A large brown stain covered one thigh of his khakis.

"You didn't have to wait up." He rolled his blue suitcase off to one side, then lowered the laptop bag beside it.

Monica put her book face-down on the reading table, next to the empty wine glass. "I wanted to see you."

They embraced and he held her tightly. She nuzzled her nose into his shirt, which smelt faintly of body odor and fried food.

"How was the drive up?"

"Pretty good, until I spilled a hot cup of coffee in my lap just outside Vacaville."

"What'd you eat?"

He shrugged his shoulders. "I haven't had dinner. I'm starving. I hardly saw daylight today. I never left the lab. The secretary ran out and got me a burger at two."

"It's not healthy, Jeff."

"I know. Those things have, like, two thousand calories."

"No, the way you're living. What you're being asked to do."

Monica poured them each a glass of wine and turned the lights down low. He sat cross-legged on the couch. Monica sank back into the recliner, the chair where she'd nursed Jacob for eighteen months. She'd slept there many evenings with her infant son in her arms.

Jeff talked about his week in San Jose, the interminable strategy meetings followed by long hours at the computer, recoding and refining programs. Tensions were high and rising. The August deadline was starting to look shaky.

"Don't tell me you're going to start spending weekends down there, too."

Frowning, he threw his hands up in the air.

"Oh my god."

"Probably every other Saturday. Just to get us over the hump. The crew down there just isn't working fast enough."

"Jeff."

"I'll be home on Sundays?"

She shook her head.

"I know you won't like it, but it's only temporary."

"Will you please stop saying that? That's like saying a prison sentence is only temporary. This is an ongoing situation that we're dealing with. It's changed the way we live our lives. It's changed our marriage."

"I know."

"Do you?"

Jeff lifted his eyebrows, then closed his eyes and sighed.

"I know it's hard on you."

"And Jacob," she said. "I really, really think we need to move into town. If I spend the summer out here alone with a toddler, I'll go nuts. Or I'll trade in my car for a pick-up truck and join the Republican Party, which amounts to the same thing."

"So put Jacob in daycare five days a week."

"That's not the point."

"Okay, don't put him in," he said, sharply. "It doesn't make any difference to me."

"I know."

They sat quietly for a minute. Then Jeff cleared his throat and said, "You want to criticize me for working? For making the money so that we can live in a house in the first place?"

"I'm not criticizing you for having a job."

"You're insinuating that I don't do my share. I'm not here enough, or something."

Monica nodded. She picked up her wine glass, rotating its stem to and fro. "You can't say no to your boss."

He looked at her for a moment, as if gauging how to take that statement.

"Look, if you think I'm happy about this San Jose thing, I'm not," he said. "If you think working for Martin is easy, it's not. There were about a dozen times this week that I almost walked out of there."

"Why didn't you?"

He threw himself back against the couch, shaking his head slowly back and forth.

"Because you want it," Monica said.

He sat in the corner of the couch looking like a marionette that had been carelessly dropped by its master.

"What do you want me to say? That I'm ambitious? Greedy? Willing to trade my home life for a so-called career?"

"Are you?"

He dropped his chin. "I don't know. I'm going to bed."

He left her there in her rocking chair, alone in the darkened living room. He hadn't asked about Jacob. He hadn't asked how her day had been. Monica took a deep breath and held it. He was tired and frustrated, she knew that. But so was she. Why did his frustration rate higher than hers? Why did his concerns about a job, about advancing himself professionally, trump hers?

Monica didn't rate. Jeff would never come out and say it, he might not even have the brain wiring to think it, but that was what it amounted to. She didn't rate. His suffering and frustration, his struggle and guilt over what he had to give up, trumped hers. Well, this was an old story, wasn't it? Right out of the middle-twentieth-century playbook, with its post-war Neanderthals and cocktail-sodden cave parties. Man on top, woman at his feet. Ugh, bring me stick.

It wasn't that she resented being a stay-at-home mom. Spending time with Jacob was wonderful. It felt vital and essential, the right thing to do. It made her feel like a good mother. But what about the other side of it? If you make that "choice," you aren't supposed to complain about what you give up. Your "free time." Your job or career. Certain circles of friends: those who, you gradually realize, have little tolerance for children (especially yours, after he spit up on their leather sofa). You give up sleep. You give up lazy afternoons in a café, reading the paper or a novel. You give up sex with your husband, or at least you give up the frequency and spontaneity of the sex. You certainly can't do it just anywhere in the house at any time of day, like you might once have done. Hell, you'll be lucky to do it in the dark, under the covers, without waking you-know-who, that funny little satellite with a sixth sense for whenever Daddy touches Mommy. All the boys think they own the rights to Mommy's body! All the boys have needs, and they depend on you, or the body that is you, to satisfy them. And a mother, a wife, must give, give, give.

As if she hadn't given enough already. Nine months of carrying a growing child around, stretching and distorting her body, crowned by the violence of birth (Jacob's delivery having been anything but smooth), leaving her torn and exhausted. She brought home a baby, a helpless infant. Monica remembered that first morning after leaving the hospital. Jeff helped to get her settled into the rocking chair in the living room of the house in Bloomington, then kissed her good-bye because he had to go and teach his eleven o'clock class, and then meet with his thesis adviser, then work in the lab. A kiss, a hug, and then out the door, the soft click of the latch resonating in her heart, closing her and Jacob in and the world out, separating her from everything she'd ever known, placing her, alone for the first time, in the newest chamber of her life. There she sat, cradling this impossibly small, helpless thing, this pink, wrinkled creature swaddled in a blanket, wearing a dainty blue cap, his hands balled up in funny little fists, looking, oddly enough, like a tiny, cranky old man. Jacob slept in her arms and Monica sat still as a statue in her chair, afraid to shift her weight for fear of waking him. She was supposed to feel warm and loving. She was supposed to feel a sunburst of affection and devotion, the immeasurable, invincible love of a mother for her child. But what grew inside her that morning was a small, icy kernel of fear. Fear and doubt. For the first time, she, a mother, was alone with her child. There was no nurse to call, just a button's push away. There was no husband to assist her. When Jacob woke and cried, as he inevitably would, it would be just her. Somehow, all the books she'd read, the parenting classes she'd attended, the helpful advice from the nurses at the hospital, the nursing coach—it wasn't enough. She wasn't ready.

A terrible, soul-contorting ache of terror tightened inside her. She sat in that chair with her infant son on that first morning home and she wept, the tears streaming down her face, dampening the neckline of her nightgown.

Those first months weren't easy for any of them. Jeff, in his final semester of graduate school, was beyond busy. When he was home, he did all he could to help. He loved to change the baby's diapers, loved to bathe him in the little yellow tub they had in the bathroom. When the baby cried at three in the morning, Jeff sprang out of bed. He loved to hold Jacob against his shoulder, burping him after a big feeding. With Jeff around, Monica always felt better, more confident and competent. But then morning came and her husband was gone, leaving mother home alone with son, and the fear and the doubt returned.

Gradually, of course, that all eased, replaced by new concerns. The mother of a toddler pines for adult conversation. The mother of a toddler recalls fondly those days when she could leave her baby on his back on a blanket on the floor while she ran to answer the phone (got to *find* it first, where in heck did she leave it?), or simply pour another cup of coffee. The mother of a toddler recalls with warmth the days when all her son could do was roll over and crawl, because then it was easy enough to plunk him in his crib or play pen, both of which he now can scale as quickly as a cat. The mother of a toddler can't take her eye off her son for long, or she'll find him chewing the mail. Or she'll find the French doors in the master bedroom open and her toddler standing on the back deck, wobbling at the lip of the steep staircase, poised for a disaster, and she will walk very carefully and slowly to him and pick him up and wrap him tightly in her arms while he laughs with oblivious glee, and she will sit herself down in a patio chair, trembling for what might have just happened. Later that day, she will drive into town and buy a sliding lock for those French doors at the hardware store, and install it herself that very night (because her husband is never home), high up and out of reach.

The mother of a toddler faces each new day with a kind of certitude: there will be a half-dozen or more diaper changes (often a wrestling match), feedings every couple of hours (often target practice for promising shot-putters), story time (don't tear the pages!), nap time (sleep, you wretch, sleep!), play time (don't throw blocks at Mommy! Say you're sorry!), and the inevitable temper tantrum (@#$%!). To be a mother meant she would never be free. Her son would always be her son, and therefore her responsibility. She would never reclaim her life as her own. To be a mother meant an erasure of the self, a radical reconfiguration of the world as you know it. A displacement, an injury, a rupture.

No one understood you if you talked like this.

8

Monica hadn't seen her mother in over a year. Claudia's face had always been lean and taut, with a healthy glow. Now it seemed paler. She wore her hair, graying at the temples, pulled back in a matronly bun. Dark spots freckled her hands and forearms. She was just sixty, though she looked older.

They spent the first day out at the house in Yolo Canyon, playing with Jacob and chatting. The morning was easy enough. Claudia sat in the rocking chair with Jacob in her lap. He leaned his round, curl-covered head against his grandmother's bosom. Despite Monica's worries, there was no thaw period. Jacob went right to his grandmother, and was content to let her hold him as much as she liked. Claudia read three *Frog and Toad* stories to him, back-to-back. Quietly, Monica was surprised. Jacob almost never did that with her. They were lucky to finish one story, let alone get started on the second. Claudia had something, who knew what, that calmed him. Kids are sensitive that way. They pick up on your body language, the tone of your voice. They can tell if you're uptight, if you're angry. They're sensitive little registers.

By that line of reasoning, Jacob should have been squirming in his grandmother's lap, thought Monica. Something isn't right here. She's charmed him. Like a witch.

After lunch, Monica put Jacob down for a nap. And though she'd told herself she wouldn't, she fell asleep with him, dozing for thirty minutes or so before she emerged from the bedroom. Monica found her mother in the kitchen, scrubbing out the sink with a can of Comet and a Brillo pad.

"You have lime deposits in your water," Claudia said, grimly.

"It's well water."

"I suppose it is. I'll take a look at your bathrooms, after this."

"Mom, I didn't ask you out here so you could clean my house. You don't have to do that."

She turned and put a hand on her hip. "Do you have any objection?"

Ah, *there* was the old Claudia! Putting you in your place, challenging you to defy her conclusion. Turning the slightest thing into a point of contest.

Monica shrugged her shoulders. "I'll be in the study, in the back."

She hadn't written much in the last two weeks. Really, it felt like starting over. She opened a draft of an essay she hadn't looked at in some time and read it. It'd been abandoned somewhere in the middle, one of those pieces she'd worked on for a week or two and then hit a dead end. It was an essay about Saundra's shoplifting phase, and of course it had to conclude with the day she got caught. Monica hadn't gotten anywhere near to writing that scene. She'd left off with Saundra standing in a shop, contemplating one item or another, plotting her escape. It ended there, with the thief fingering her goods.

On re-reading the draft, Monica thought she felt a certain snap and pull to the language. It still seemed like something worth working on. (That August deadline for graduate school hovered in the back of her mind.) If she needed any further motivation, she need only glance to the bookshelf beside her desk to see the recently-acquired Oates novel tucked between its cousins like a stowaway. Perhaps she'd stolen that book for a reason, after all.

She settled in with her cup of coffee and began to type.

Two hours later, she was interrupted by a light knocking on the study door. "Yes?"

Claudia opened it, a sleepy Jacob in her arms, leaning his head against his grandmother's shoulder, a blue pacifier plugged in his mouth like a drain stop.

"Somebody wants to see his Mommy," Claudia said, smiling.

"Hi, honeybunch! Mommy didn't hear you wake up."

"We were very quiet," Claudia said.

Monica saved her document and snapped the laptop shut. She held her arms out, and Claudia brought Jacob to her. He curled up in her lap. Monica ran her hands through his fine, soft hair.

"What were you working on?" Claudia asked.

"An essay."

"Your memoir."

Monica cleared her throat.

"Am I going to see more of it?"

"When it's finished." Monica bounced Jacob on her knee. "Can I ask you a question about something? Do you remember that time Saundra got hauled into the manager's office for shoplifting? What do you remember about that, exactly?"

Claudia lifted her chin. Her lips shrank and became thin.

"The man was a brute. Terrorizing a young girl like that."

"But she had stolen from the store."

"Yes." Claudia folded her arms. "You're not writing about that, are you? Let the dead keep their secrets."

"I don't know what you're afraid of," Monica said. "Saundra wouldn't mind. I used to hear her tell that story to friends."

"What's behind this drive to bare our family secrets?"

"I'm writing a memoir. What's the point of a memoir unless you share a secret or two?"

"The trouble is the lines you cross. What you write about your sister, who can't respond. Or your father. Or me."

"I guess you'll just have to trust me."

Claudia screwed up her lip and nodded.

The next day, Monica put Jacob in daycare and took her mother into town. They sat in a busy Starbucks along a tree-lined avenue called the Esplanade (rhyming, in the local parlance, with lemonade). Just weeks ago, Monica told her mother, the building had been a French *patisserie*—the only genuine *patisserie* in Chico. And though Monica certainly loved her Starbucks, it saddened her to see a unique, mom-and-pop store like that gobbled up by the latest mega-chain. Starbucks, Costco, Bank of America: what could you do? Monica mentioned a recent news story that had upset her, a story about union-breaking practices at Wal-Mart. Every time the underpaid high school kids or the retirees tried to unionize, the bigwigs stepped in and bullied them. Meanwhile, the company was trying to build a second store in Chico. A few angry voices had been raised, but Monica figured the corporation would win in the end. Seriously, what could you do?

Claudia sighed. "It's the kind of fight I always imagined your sister might take on."

"Mom, please. Saundra worked for a law firm that backed major pharmaceutical companies. She specialized in medical patent law. You can't crawl much deeper inside the machine than that."

"She was doing what was required to learn her trade. She would have gotten inside, seen how it worked, then acted from a position of authority and knowledge."

"Saundra wanted to be rich, not socially useful."

Claudia frowned. "It is possible to be both materially wealthy and morally correct."

"Except that money and power both corrupt." Monica blew on her Americano with soy milk. "Saundra wasn't a bad person. She just wasn't extraordinarily good. She wanted a lakeshore home in a gated community. She wanted a BMW."

"I had no idea you were so cynical about your sister."

"That's not being cynical. I'm being honest."

"Is that what you call it."

Monica gave a little huff, crossed her arms across her chest. "What would you call it?"

Claudia reached across for a bite of muffin. She chewed and swallowed, taking her time. "I want to ask you a question. Will you answer it honestly?"

"Maybe."

"Were you jealous of her?"

Monica lifted her chin. "That's totally absurd. Like I wanted to go to law school and be a lawyer? Like I lust after money? Look at my house. Look at my car. Give me a break."

"I don't mean in that way."

"Then how?"

Monica glanced out the window at the passing cars, bracing herself for whatever zinger Claudia had been waiting to unload.

"You know, on second thought," Monica said, "let's not go there."

Her mother lowered her gaze to the table. "I don't understand why you're writing that book."

"You don't have to understand. It's not your book, it's mine."

"You're making a mistake."

"How do you know?"

They sat across the table from one another, not meeting each other's eyes.

"Go on, say it," Monica said, sharply. "It's what I usually do."

Claudia leaned forward and hissed, "Why don't you grow up!"

Monica felt anger and frustration welling inside, like dark clouds gathering for a tempest. Finally, she blurted out, "Jesus Christ!" and slapped the table forcefully. She stood from the table.

"I'll be in the car."

And she stormed out of the shop.

A few minutes later, Claudia joined her. They sat quietly side-by-side, staring out the front window at the cars passing on the busy street. Red light, the cars backed up in lines; green light, they drove off, making their various turns, every one of them on some kind of mission.

"You're not worried about Saundra, or Jacob," Monica said. "You're worried about you. What I might say about you."

Her mother brushed the knee of her skirt. "I'm afraid I won't be able to forgive you."

"Don't worry, I won't *embarrass* you," Monica said, sharply. "You'll be dead and gone before anyone reads my book."

She'd meant to say that she was an impossibly slow writer, that it would be years before her book would be complete. But she sensed, in an instant, that her mother had taken it another way.

"Mom, I'm sorry, I didn't mean—"

"—That's fine. I know perfectly well how you feel." She uttered a deep, protracted sigh. "Your sister was a loyal daughter, and a genuine confidante. She reported on most of your conversations."

Monica thought about that for a moment. "Not as often as you think."

"More often than you know."

Monica gripped the steering wheel between both hands, squeezing and releasing, feeling its firm, slightly spongy texture. The sisters had always breached little confidences, sharing others' secrets with one another and demanding a vow of silence. Monica knew it had been no different between Saundra and Claudia. They had always had a tight bond, something inscrutable and mysterious to Monica, who'd always felt like a bit of an outsider in her own home, despite being surrounded by family, by women.

"Well, it worked both ways," Monica muttered.

"I know it did," Claudia said. "That's why I never said anything to your sister that I didn't want repeated. And there were plenty of things I did want repeated. I could always count on your sister. She could tell you things that you wouldn't have suffered from my lips."

"Like what?"

"Oh, a million things."

"Just name one."

Claudia crossed her arms.

"It was through your sister that I learned why you'd *really* dropped out of college. And it was through her that I got you to re-enroll, after you'd abandoned that absurd rock music thing."

"She had nothing to do with that," Monica said, quickly.

"She most certainly did. You talked to her several times. She presented you with good reasons why you needed to complete your degree. She gave you encouragement and deadlines. She motivated you when you had no motivation."

"Saundra wanted me to major in business. And she wanted me to transfer to Northwestern, to finish up there."

"So she could keep an eye on you."

"She was working sixty hours a week!"

"She always made time for you."

A goldfinch hopped about in the empty parking spot to her left, pecking at stray bits of waste.

"I'd already re-enrolled by the time she was grilling me," Monica said.

"You hadn't committed," Claudia insisted. "You were wavering. You needed guidance and assurance."

"I'd already re-enrolled," Monica repeated, firmly. She gripped and re-gripped the steering wheel in her hands. "I did that right after my abortion."

Claudia turned in her seat. "What?"

Monica met her mother's gaze. She felt her eyes filling, felt a cold twisting of the heart.

In a soft voice, she said, "She told you everything, did she."

With a huff, Claudia turned away, one hand clasped around a wrist.

Monica slid her keys into the car's ignition. She had some trouble turning them, the mechanism being old and temperamental. One day, she supposed, the car just wouldn't start.

But the key turned, finally, and the engine coughed to life. Monica drove slowly through the tight, congested parking lot, looking for an exit. They were never where they should be.

Another poopy diaper, another soiled outfit. As she lifted Jacob up onto the changing table, Monica swore she'd never feed her toddler broccoli and carrots with cheese ever again. His diarrhea confirmed that her own life-long aversion to the green vegetable was not simply a matter of taste, as her mother argued, but a genetic predisposition against it—one that, sadly, she'd passed on to her son. Well, now they knew. From that moment forward, broccoli was verboten in her house.

Monica wiped Jacob clean as quickly as she could while dodging his flailing legs and arms, then reached a hand down below, blindly groping for a clean diaper. Of course, there were none. She'd forgotten to restock after the last blowout. And so she put her son on the floor to let him run around bare-ass naked while she hunted for a clean diaper. The closest one would be in her shoulder bag, so Monica followed Jacob out into the living room, intent on digging a hand into her overstuffed bag. And that is where she found her mother on the couch, a small pile of manuscript pages beside her, holding one typewritten sheet up before her, eyes narrowed.

"What have you got there?" Monica asked.

Claudia lowered the manuscript page. Her eyes were red and wet.

"A 'tyrant and a bitch'?"

"What?"

From the pile beside her, Claudia tugged at a few sheets of paper, sorted odd-ways, jutting out from the pile. She held one up and read from it, "A 'brazen manipulator,'" then tossed the sheet with a flick of the wrist, sending it fluttering to the floor. She reached for another sheet. "'Queen Bitch.'" Another. "'Dried up old shrew.'" She flicked a fingertip against the pile. "I haven't even gotten thirty pages into this thing."

Monica rushed forward and snatched the page out of her mother's hand. "What in *hell* are you doing with my manuscript?"

Her mother sat straight-backed and chin high. "I knew what you were doing. I knew you would be ungenerous and critical, you with your little axe to grind, having it out with me on the page. Don't you think that everyone will see right through you, see you for the petty, complaining wretch you are?"

"I'm not a wretch," Monica said, reaching down to collect the manuscript from the couch. "You had no right to snoop around like that, no right to read my work. I told you it wasn't ready."

"It won't be ready until I'm dead and gone," her mother snapped. She stood from the couch. "You're a coward."

Monica straightened, the manuscript mis-sorted and uneven in her arms. Stray pages littered the couch cushion and the floor. Her mother stood before her, arms crossed, hands dug tightly into the crooks of her elbows.

"And you're a dirty snoop," Monica said. "For a woman your age, someone who pretends to be so tough and clear-minded, you're remarkably insecure."

The slap came fast. Monica, with the manuscript in her arms, couldn't possibly have dodged it even if she'd wanted to—which she did not. A rosy, hot, pins-and-needles sting grew on her cheek.

"Do you feel better now?" she mocked.

"I feel horrible!" her mother shouted, and bolted out of the room, heading for the guest bedroom in the back. The door slammed shut heavily. Monica collected the loose sheets of her manuscript. Behind her, she heard the familiar thumping of her son's feet.

"Mama." His voice sounded plaintive, sad. She turned and saw him naked, his calves and ankles covered in slick, wet diarrhea.

"Oh my god," she blurted, dropping the manuscript onto the coffee table, where it toppled, the pages sliding onto the floor in a messy, disjointed bunch. She quickly picked Jacob up, lifting him by the armpits, and dashed for the tub. He began to cry. The little guy had had an accident, he'd made a mess on the floor, and it was her fault. She knew her son was ashamed, that he was worried what his mother would say. She cleaned him quickly, washing him in warm, soapy water, and reassured him. It wasn't his fault, she told him. Mommy got distracted. He'd done nothing wrong. Accidents happen, and Mommy loves him, and please, please, please stop your crying.

9

After the manuscript incident, Monica and Claudia hardly spoke to one another. Thankfully, Jeff arrived home later the next day, Saturday, and whipped together a big, jolly dinner. Sensing tension between mother and daughter, he picked up the slack, chatting breezily with his mother-in-law, making up for the many hours he'd been away, taking everyone's minds off the tension and unease. Monica distracted herself with her son, bathing him, reading him book after book. Claudia drank too much wine at dinner and put herself to bed early.

The next morning, Monica and Jacob dropped Claudia off at the Chico airport, lingering to watch her go through the tiny security checkpoint and then walk out onto the airstrip and climb up the steps of the commuter plane. Jacob thumped his plump palm against the glass and stomped his feet, chanting "Nana! Nana! Nana!" like an incantation. Monica would've given anything to be inside his little brain, his little heart, at that moment, because it wasn't love she felt, nor nostalgia nor longing, but only relief and regret, in more-or-less equal measures. It would be a long time, she knew, before she and her mother would see one another again.

Driving out of the airport, Monica did not turn left toward Yolo Canyon. It was mid-afternoon, a pleasant day, and she felt like being around people. And so she drove to the mall, where she strapped Jacob into his stroller and arranged, on the tray before him, a juice box and a little cup of animal crackers.

Ah, to stroll the air-conditioned promenade with the retirees in their off-brand walking shoes, taking their exercise. And the portly housewives. And the teens hanging around the video game store: the chubby-cheeked girls with make-up caked on their faces, and the skinny white boys trying to look like gangstas, with their bluejeans halfway down their ass. (They're probably all high on meth, and more power to 'em! A waste is a terrible thing to mind.) And the mothers of newborns and toddlers, Monica's tribe, pushing their strollers, moving sometimes three abreast, like some strange street parade. Monica pushed her son in his stroller up and down the hallways, poking into a few stores. She rarely purchased things at the mall unless they were on a sales rack. But on that afternoon, she found herself browsing, eyeing expensive things: silk blouses, Italian leather pumps, designer handbags. In a back aisle of Victoria's Secret, Monica fingered a pair of lacy underwear. All the clothing had clunky anti-theft devices stapled to it, but not this pair of underwear. And it was Monica's size. And it was a pearlescent gray—skimpy, impractical, and wildly overpriced, but sort of gorgeous.

She stood in the back aisle, gently rubbing the velvety fabric between index finger and thumb, thinking about Saundra and how she must have planned her heists. Monica had always assumed that the thefts were impulsive, hasty, and rash, desperate affairs of luck and timing. She understood now how wrong she'd been. The best shoplifter is cool and calculating. She scopes out exits, takes note of security cameras, and above all watches what the clerks and customers are doing. She feels the dark, intoxicating rush building in the stomach and radiating outwards, the tingle of adrenaline, the heightened awareness: a predator studying its prey, locked in and alive. Totally in the moment. It's better than any drug, better than the Dexedrine she's been filching out of her mother's cabinet, better than the cigarettes she's been choking on behind the high school gymnasium. It is a secret, a bad decision, a small, dark wound.

Reaching down, Monica stuffed the underwear deep into a pocket of Jacob's diaper bag. Even then, she was anything but hasty. She walked slowly through the store, still browsing. She coolly made her way out the door, through the upright scanner, the thing that would have blurted and beeped and buzzed if it had detected a thief exiting the store.

Walking for her car, Monica felt the secret rush of adrenalin begin to ebb. She told herself it felt wrong *and* exciting, perverted *and* glorious, that she was glad she'd done it *and* disgusted with herself all at once, just as Saundra might have felt. Just as she had felt after lying to her mother about the abortion. Every woman has her secret inner life, her dark chamber of errors, mistakes, regrets. Maybe being a writer is just finding a way to use that stuff productively.

In the car, driving up the Esplanade, out of town, Jacob quickly gave in to the tidal pull of sleep, clutching his beloved hammer tightly in his little, meaty fist. Monica, willing herself to feel giddy and excited, drove home a little faster than usual. She felt like opening a bottle of wine, calling up a girlfriend.

At home she put Jacob into his crib, and then she did open that bottle of wine: a chilled pinot grigio from Sonoma County. Halfway into her second glass, she collected her other pilfered item, the Oates novel. Another book about troubled teens. Something didn't look right about the book—the jacket art suddenly seemed tacky and jejune. Did she even want to read this thing?

And then the lacy underwear. Why gray? Why a thong? She'd never worn a thong. Holding the goods in her hand, she tried to muster up a little nervous excitement, a little rush. But it was impossible.

And then it hit her. That's good! That's perfect! That's what she didn't know!

Every thief feels let down after a haul. That made sense. It was the deed itself, the moment of committing the crime, that brought on the rush. What followed could only be a let-down. Like a drunkard reaching for the next drink, the kleptomaniac's only solace came in repeating the crime, each new act a pathetic attempt to recapture what was lost. A logic of diminishing returns.

Monica understood something new about Saundra, how she'd felt these ups-and-downs, these mood swings. She reached for her Moleskine notebook, which she now carried in her shoulder bag at all times, and scribbled a few hasty notes for later.

Then, from the back of the house, the creak of floorboards. A soft footstep.

Monica leapt out of her chair, book and underwear in one hand, and rushed into the back room. Maybe, she thought, if she got there a little sooner, she'd see something more than that shoulder, that yellow shirt. She hurtled through the baby's room, the sun room, exploding into the study.

But she saw nothing. No shoulder, no human form at all. Just the still, blue room in the soft light of dusk, with her husband's books and papers scattered around. She studied the room carefully, trying to be open to whatever she should be feeling.

"Are you there? Who are you? What do you want?"

From the baby's room, Jacob cried out, "Momma!" One of them had woken him, with her stomping around. She hesitated, trying to sense something, anything, any kind of answer. In the far, upper corner of the room, a spider lowered itself on a single silken strand, then stopped and hovered, mid-air, twirling.

Monica placed the book and the panties in a neat stack on a cushion of the worn loveseat. "Here. These are for you."

She lingered a moment longer, hoping for some sign, some recognition. The spider twirled and dangled, a dancer lost in space.

Monica, restless and unable to sleep, stayed up, waiting for Jeff and writing, working on the shoplifting essay. She'd written a few good pages, had recorded the languor from which the desire arose, the steady build-up, the growing certainty of it, an irresistible urge that led Saundra, despite the gnawing of her conscience, to move toward a store. Then the heady rush of entering, a slight trembling in the hands and gut, the nervous anticipation quickly giving way to a preternatural calm and clarity, Saundra now slipping into the familiar groove, the sense of infallibility, the command of the moment. She found the item she wanted most, walked with it casually in her hand, stopping to browse other items, taking her time, not calling attention to herself. And then finding the right spot, the right corner of the store, the exact preferred moment as she slipped the item under a shirt or in a pocket with a quick, practiced gesture, smooth and unobtrusive. Or, as Saundra had done on that fateful day, boldly slipping on a pair of Ray-Ban sunglasses walking for the exit. Oh, the rush of *that!* She'd done it a dozen times or more and never been caught. Then the rotund guard clearing his throat, calling out "Miss, excuse me," and a firm hand on her upper arm….

That's where Monica hit another wall. It should be easy to write that final scene, she thought. The confrontation and threats, the manager leering over her, yelling in her face. The fear and shame, burning her, scarring her, blinding her. Curing her.

Jeff got home early on Friday, looking haggard and worn, but in good spirits. From his suitcase and pulled out a brown paper bag, from which he took a bottle of Rioja, a Tempranillo they were both fond of, along with a brick of Spanish manchego and a package of prosciutto.

"How about a glass of wine?"

She smiled. "What's the occasion?"

"Our move into town. Or should I say, 'a town.'"

Monica gave him a puzzled look.

The firm in San Jose had taken him out to lunch that afternoon, Jeff explained, and offered him a job. He would oversee the programming end of the website on a permanent basis.

"Sort of figured this was coming. They can't live without me, that's obvious. I'm too deeply invested, got my fingers in every pot. Sort of made sure of that. And they love me, they absolutely love me."

"Oh my god," she said, shaking her head. "You want to move to San Jose."

He smiled and nodded. "What do you say? We could be living there in two weeks!"

"What about this place?"

Jeff snapped his fingers. "They're going to help us out."

The company would assume the mortgage in Yolo Canyon, he said, until they could find a buyer. In the meantime, Jeff's cohorts had recommended a short list of brokers in the San Jose area.

"Housing is out of control down there, so I don't know," he said. "But I think maybe you're right: we just have to jump in and start swimming. Maybe rent for a while, I don't know. We'll figure it out."

He threw himself back on the couch.

"That's if we take it," he said. "If you agree. It's going to be different."

"Different is good," Monica said. "I can live with different. This place…."

She fluttered a hand around, like a trapped bird.

"I know."

"You haven't told Martin?"

"No, of course not. You're the first, babe." Jeff ran a hand through his hair. "Martin will freak out. He had big plans for our next project."

Jeff talked about that briefly, about his feelings of gratitude and debt to the guy who'd given him his first job, who'd trusted in his talent and ability, who'd lured him out to the West Coast to become part of the biggest IT explosion ever. But the best of it was happening in Silicon Valley, that's where the real trend-setters and pioneers were working. If a guy were going to make The Big Leap, that was where he should land. Martin had to understand that. And if he didn't, well, hey, that's business. Jeff had put in more than a year there, given his share.

He picked up the brick of manchego. "This cheese has to be cut, and soon."

"I'll get a knife," she said.

"I'll go toss these bags in my office." He walked off through the doorway, into the back.

Monica got two wine glasses and the opener, a wooden board and knife for the cheese, and a small plate for the prosciutto. This was their favorite Spanish tapa. Jeff's news, while sudden, cheered her. It wasn't the change she'd imagined, not exactly. When she'd thought of moving to town, she'd thought of Chico, a lovely little college town with gorgeous, tree-lined avenues and quaint neighborhoods. And her mall. She'd only been to San Jose once, when she took Jacob to the Children's Museum. Her impressions were not flattering: generic urban sprawl; yuppie programmers like her husband in shiny German imports clogging up the freeways; spoiled white kids spray-painting under the bridges.

But the Bay Area was a mecca, all the way up the peninsula and into San Francisco. And there were so many good schools there, so many places Monica could finish her degree. Museums for Jacob. Concerts. She wouldn't need any malls!

The life that could be built there was without limits, she really felt that. Or at least she felt willing to try.

Jeff returned with the Oates book in one hand and the lacy underwear and the blouse in the other.

"Are these yours?"

Monica bit her lower lip. "They're a gift for somebody."

"Who?"

She stepped forward and took the items from his hand.

Jeff tugged on the lacy underwear. "I was sort of hoping you got these for you."

Monica smiled. "Maybe I did."

"I thought you said they were a gift."

"I didn't say for who," she said, reaching over and turning off the light. "Let's see if they fit."

Jeff touched her arm, caressed her shoulder gently. She stepped closer. He wrapped an arm around her and pulled her close. She buried her nose in his neck, brushing her lips lightly against his skin, then began to kiss him, softly. His hand moved up and down her back, tracing her spine. His fingertips dipped just inside the waist of her bluejeans. She ran her hands along his taut arms.

"Should we move to the bedroom?" he asked in a whisper, his breath hot in her ear.

"No. Right here."

He unbuttoned her blouse slowly, removing first the left shoulder, then the right. He brushed his tongue against her skin. Monica reached around, unfastening her bra with a practiced move, slipping out of it quickly. Jeff knelt and kissed her belly, her ribs, kissed the underside of her breasts, ran his tongue between them, across them. Monica ran her fingers through his hair. Then he stood and kissed her again.

They moved to the couch. His hand caressed every curve, fingertips light as butterflies. She felt a growing warmth, the ineluctable swelling of a wave, an ocean wave coursing over her glowing body, crashing ashore in a tremendous tumult, spilling over the warm sand, spreading itself over every grain, hovering for a moment before sinking back into the sea.

10

The next morning, after a leisurely breakfast with husband and son, Monica went into her bedroom and began to plan the day's adventure. She dressed in a simple yellow dress and wide-brimmed straw hat, both of which she'd picked up at a thrift shop a week earlier in anticipation of this day. A day when Jeff would be at home with their son. A day when a girl could roam.

She pulled on light hose, something she never wore. But then she wasn't herself. She was a walking experiment, a daring challenge on two legs.

She stood before the mirror, applying a bit of powder and some lipstick. Nothing bold or brassy, just a touch of color. She adjusted her neckline and the angle of her hat. There, just like that, Monica became Monique.

In the living room, Jeff sat on the floor, wearing an old Indiana University T-shirt, the lettering faded and cracked. Jacob lay on his belly, playing with wooden blocks. His father patiently stacked them for him, and then Jacob, giggling, knocked them down with his beloved hammer.

Jeff studied her. His eyes narrowed, then widened.

"You're going to a quilting show," he said.

She shook her head.

"Visiting a gallery."

Nope.

"Then you must be robbing a bank." He gathered the fallen blocks and began to build another tower. "To tell you the truth, we could probably use a boost for that down payment in San Jose."

She did not answer him, distracted by the pattern of sunlight on the wooden paneling in the kitchen.

"Everything okay?" Jeff asked.

She clicked her heels together and straightened.

Everything is fine, she told him, she just wanted one afternoon to herself to be someone other than who she was. Call it an experiment, a few hours in a funny outfit, wandering around town, trying to find something out.

"Find out what?"

"It's research for my book," she said. "Don't ask questions. You'll kill the mood."

"All right. Have fun and don't get arrested."

She paused at the front door. "You'll be home?"

"We might go down by the creek. Looks like a nice day for tadpole hunting."

"It is a nice day," she said. "It's a lovely day. Just have your cell phone with you. And have it on, okay?"

"Are you anticipating trouble?"

She twirled the strap of the enormous black bag she carried over her shoulder. "Nothing but!"

In the department store, she wandered through the densely-packed aisles of the women's section, slowly collecting items. Things she needed, things she might actually want. This should be real, she reminded herself. No faking it. And so she collected blouses and leg ware for herself, along with a lacy black bra. From the girl's section, she took a lovely summer dress for Jacob. And from the home living section, a new vegetable peeler, and a pewter martini shaker—something for Jeff.

At the front of the store, she stood before the check-out lines, feigning distraction as she girded herself for what must follow. And then she did it: she stepped forward, making for the front door. As she passed through a series of upright security gates, a beeper sounded—rapid, annoying, like a bug zapper on steroids. Heads turned all around her, suddenly the object of attention. She made eye contact with one of the store employees, then stepped toward the door.

"Miss!" a strong, matronly voice sounded from one of the check-out lanes.

She hurried her pace. A portly security guard, complete with ill-fitting polyester uniform and wannabe-cop buzzcut, double-timed it after her. Monica bolted out the door, jogging sloppily along the sidewalk, caroming off a stack of bagged mulch. She had just stepped off the curb, headed for the vast, black expanse of the half-empty parking lot when she felt the firm grip on her upper arm. The security guard barked in her ear to stop. She turned to him, laughing.

The store manager's office was a grubby little box of a room with a window looking out onto a vast warehouse. The door, gray with fingerprints around the battered handle, slammed shut behind her with a hollow, thin sound. The manager was a short, chubby man with a half-ring of dark hair around the back of his otherwise bald head. He wore a pair of narrow, Euro-style eyeglasses that did not compliment him. The items from Monica's shoulder bag were spread across his desk.

"You like a strong cocktail," he said, holding up the martini shaker. "Quite a haul here, Miss…."

As he looked up, his eyes seemed beady and small behind the spectacles.

"Saunders," she said. "Monique Saunders."

"Well, it all adds up to a pretty penny, Monique, that's for sure."

He sat back in his chair, which uttered a loud creak as its weight shifted.

"Can you give me one reason why I shouldn't call the police right now?"

"Yes. You're supposed to scold me first."

"No, this is the part where you give me the phony sob story. You know, you're suffering a migraine. Your boyfriend cheated on you. You're off your meds."

Monica cleared her throat, then said, "My sister died."

The manager motioned with a hand for her to continue.

She rubbed her hands along the plastic arms of her chair.

"It was a spring evening, a beautiful, clear night. She was out for a drink, sitting on the back patio of a trendy downtown bar with a friend. My sister looked up at the sky, thought how it looked like a piece of fabric stretched between the tops of the tall buildings, a jeweled city under an indigo dome."

Overly florid, she thought. But a start. Just keep going.

"She only wanted to be happy in this life, to be grateful for everything she'd earned or been given. But she'd failed an important exam. Her bosses worked her like a slave, no respite. And her boyfriend, the one she'd thought might be The One, had recently moved to another town. He'd put his career first and was climbing like a rocket. My sister felt like a distant second on his list. My sister felt alone, she felt stuck, she felt miserable. She spilled her heart out to her friend as they ordered drink after drink, but it wasn't helping. Instead of lifting, her mood fell. The friend began to worry. The friend began to feel uncomfortable. My sister seemed more than sad. She seemed… embroiled in melancholy."

Monica banged a fist against her knee.

"No, not melancholy. Scratch that. What's another word for melancholy?"

The store manager lifted his eyebrows. "I'm sorry?"

"Gloom. Misery. Despair."

Monica sat for a moment, thinking. No better word came to her, and anyway it was only a word. The words can be, will be revised later.

"What are you talking about?"

"My sister," said Monica, sitting forward. "The friend was worried. She guided my sister out of there, hailed a cab, paid for it to take her back to Evanston. But this was a mistake. Alone, with no one and nothing to hold back the… the… the melancholy."

"Miss Saunders, you're not exactly answering my question."

Monica held up a hand.

"The apartment was dark, still, sepulchral. She wanted to sleep. She wanted the deepest, longest sleep, wanted to wake up and have everything seem new, a fresh start. She poured herself a glass of gin. She took a sleeping pill, then another. And another. She stood for several minutes with the open bottle of pills in her hand, everything oddly narrowed to whatever she chose to do next.

"Finally, she swallowed a handful of pills. She collapsed into bed. A darkness swirled around her, enfolding her, sort of like drowning. They say when you drown the first minute is horrible, but then a terrific peace comes over you, a sense of wellbeing. That's how I want to imagine my sister as she lay alone in that apartment, in the dark. Her last thoughts."

Monica sat quietly for a moment, pausing like the white space between sections of an essay.

"I've tried to remember the last time I spoke to her. We argued about what to buy my mother for her birthday. We were going to split the cost, whatever it was, but we couldn't agree. We couldn't agree."

She sat back in her chair, fiddling with the hem of her dress.

The store manager tapped a ballpoint pen against his wrist.

"Are we finished?"

Monica nodded.

"Well, I have to admit, this is new. I've never had anyone claim that they stole as a form of bereavement."

"But it's the truth."

"I don't know." The manager shook his head very slowly. "And frankly, I don't care. I could call the cops and make a big brouhaha out of this, but as it happens my plate is full. It's your lucky day. I'm willing to forget this happened. I want you to leave now, Miss Saunders. Turn around and go home. Just promise me you won't step foot in the store ever again, all right?"

"No," Monica said. "No, you can't let me off the hook. You need to be angry. You need to threaten me with the cops or something."

"What?"

She stood from her chair.

"I need you at your worst. I want fury, rage... no, I want outrage!"

The manager narrowed his eyes, then removed his glasses and pressed the base of his hands into his eye sockets.

"You're not the first headache of the day, you know," he said, slowly. "Try one employee caught stealing and a floor manager drunk on the job. Both fired, naturally. And because I sacked a junior manager I'm here until ten o'clock tonight, which means I'll miss my daughter's dance recital. So forgive me if I am not moved by your rather sad story. Which, quite honestly, I don't know if I believe. I do know you're not a thief. In my ten years at this store I've had, I don't know, a couple dozen of these encounters. I know a shoplifter when I see one. You may have problems, but you're no klepto. So do us both a favor. Just turn around and walk off with no further reprimand, no call to the police, no temper tantrum. Just leave. Leave so that this day can be that much closer to its end and so that I can go home to my wife and daughter, who surely will understand me as everyone else today has not."

"But you see—"

The manager thumped his fists against his desktop.

"Leave!" he bellowed. "Leave, or by God I will call the cops!"

Monica smiled, studying the man's grimace, his angry, jutting finger. The widened eyes.

"Yes, thank you. I'm going now."

She rose from her chair and left his office, walking upright, erect, her bag empty and her heart open.

She finished the shoplifting essay a couple of weeks after that. She read it over several times. Here, she thought, is a writing sample. Here is a genuine essay. Still, she couldn't be absolutely sure—that old self-doubt so strong. She put it away in the drawer. A week later, she re-read it. She was convinced it was her best work to date, a kind of breakthrough. And before she could talk herself out of it, she dropped the manuscript into an envelope (along with a SASE for a response, of course), addressed it to the editor of a journal she respected, and sealed it up.

Monica drove downtown to the post office and mailed it off that very day, with no sentiment or hesitation. She'd mailed submissions off before, back in graduate school. Nothing had ever been accepted for publication, and when she'd dropped out of school she'd stopped sending things out, just as she'd stopped writing. But she knew about the waiting. The waiting had begun, but it was the right kind of waiting. She had other essays to write while she waited.

And she had other missions. She'd intended to return the Oates novel to the bookstore, or 'fess up and pay for the darn thing, but on second thought she decided neither would be right. She'd stolen it, for whatever reason. She'd made an offering of it once and had been repaid, she felt, in the kindest of manners. There was something to that. She stopped at a local coffee shop that had a book exchange, a take-one-leave-one affair. She sat and drank a cup of coffee and flipped through the local paper. She studied a spattering of sunlight on the brick wall. "Heroes" by David Bowie played on the café stereo, a song she'd not heard in ages, a song that made her wistful and nostalgic. When it ended, she placed her empty coffee mug into its receiving bin. On her way out she tucked the Oates novel into a bookshelf, snug and tight, a safe place to rest before finding a new home.

INFIDELS

1

In the dead of a Minnesota winter my father announced that he'd bought tickets for the demolition ice race at Malosky Stadium, where the UMD Bulldogs played football. Just the boys. My mother had no interest in watching a bunch of cars run around in a circle. That was no sport, she said airily, though she was never a sports enthusiast to begin with.

I'd never been to a car race of any sort, let alone a demolition race. The thought of watching a bunch of cars slipping and sliding around on ice, smashing into each other—I had to admit, it sounded enticing.

Dad assured me we'd have fun. In Hibbing, where he'd grown up, this was big stuff. Up there, they held a regular Grand Prix on ice. Serious racing. They had a whole season. You knew the teams and the drivers. The paper printed the standings. All the kids went, he said. He'd taken more than one girl out for a night at the races.

"That's Hibbing for you," my mother quipped. "Be glad you were born in Duluth, Jackie Rose. There are more places to take girls."

"And more girls to take," my father added. "Willing girls."

My mother folded her arms across her stomach. "Oh, you're so clever."

"I'm just saying."

"Yet not. So subtle."

My parents exchanged glances.

I looked confusedly between them. "I don't get it."

"You're not supposed to get it," my mother said.

"I'm the one who's supposed to get it," my father said, "but I'm not, and there's your problem."

Flashing a withering smile, my mother said, "That hole is getting deeper, Carl."

"I'll take any hole I can get."

My mother ordered me upstairs. Time to play my 45 rpm records, washing out the thundering drone of yet another argument.

The night before the race a light snow fell. The forecast was for sub-zero temperatures overnight, with the mercury hovering in the teens the following day. My mother worried about wind chill and frostbite.

"You can do any damn fool thing you like on a winter's day," she said to my father, "but dragging Jackie outdoors on a day like this…. It's foolish. It's dangerous."

Dad assured her we'd be dressed warmly, in layers, that we'd probably only be outside for an hour anyway.

"Jackie's a tough kid. You're pumped for this, aren't you?"

Suddenly the kitchen felt like no man's land. Saying yes (or no) would please one parent but vex the other. Trying to steer a middle course I reminded both parties that, having played outdoor hockey my entire life, I was no stranger to freezing cold temperatures.

"There you go!" my father bellowed, as if he'd won a great point.

The next morning Mom fussed over me as I dressed. The temperature was in the single digits, she informed me, and wouldn't climb much higher. Double-up, wear two of everything. Keep your ears, nose, and mouth covered at all times. Frostbite can strike in mere minutes.

I wore two pairs of socks inside a pair of knockoff moon boots we'd found at JC Penney's. I wore long underwear and insulated ski pants, and above that, two shirts under a turtleneck and a wool Norwegian fisherman's sweater. On my head I wore my Minnesota North Stars green knit cap and a long scarf which I wrapped around my neck and head like a swami mystic.

My father wore his polar boots—big, clunky things with lug soles and insulation inserts as thick as your thumb. A parka, wool cap, and thick, padded leather mittens completed the look.

"Perfect conditions. This is going to be one hell of a race!" he predicted, slapping his mittens together like a seal.

During the drive over, the Pontiac's wheezing defroster struggled to keep two oval patches of glass clear on the front windshield. The passenger window was blanketed in frost. At a stop light my father took a quick nip from the flask in his coat pocket.

"Hmm," he grunted. He held the flask out. "This'll warm ya. Have a nip, Jackie."

I waved it off. I'd made the mistake of sampling his whiskey last Christmas, again at his invitation. The burn raked my throat, leaving a trail of fire down to my belly. He'd laughed, saying something about the look on my face, and I'd run out of the room cursing him.

My father refused to pay two dollars to park at the stadium, which meant we had to park a few blocks away and hoof it. Sidewalks were a mess, yesterday's slushy footprints now frozen hard as concrete. Already I was having second thoughts. A nasty north wind blew without recess, its icy fingers reaching down my neck and up the sleeves of my coat despite all my layers and wrappings.

A modest crowd peppered the bleachers of Malosky Stadium. Along the far side of the stands snowdrifts lay piled up against the walls, covering several seats. My father bought us cups of hot chocolate and hot dogs, which proved difficult to eat with all our clothing. After the second bite the hot dog was cold anyway, a spongy flaccid tube of mystery meat.

Before us, on the field where I'd watched the Bulldogs play football in the autumn, and where I'd cavorted during summer sports camp, a massive figure-8 track of ice had been poured, stretching between end zones and meeting midfield. A dozen battered old cars—mostly mid-Sixties coupes and sedans, or older—stood in lines. Their bodies, covered in dents and bashes, had been painted garish reds and oranges and purples. The side panels advertised local towing services, bail bondsmen, and salvage companies. Stripped of all glass, chrome, and external hardware, their spiked ice tires bristling, the cars looked fierce and primal.

At the announcer's bidding, engines roared to life, belching black plumes of exhaust. My dad and I placed mock bets on who would win. He was sure it would be one of the juggernauts: Number 17, a bulky Chevy Impala, or Number 88, a battered Plymouth Duster. He was probably right, but I had my eye on Number 6, a forlorn Datsun 510, which might be nimble enough to dart and weave around the giants. I had my hopes.

With a wave of the green flag, they were off with a roar. Tires spun, seeking purchase. The herd charged into the first corner, jostling for position, the larger cars shouldering their way forward, but on the first turn it was clear that the spiked tires could only grip so much. Cars fishtailed and swerved, colliding with each other, careening off snowbanks and retaining walls. A purple Ford took a shot from behind and was sent spinning off into a corner, where its hood popped open and smoke began billowing from the engine. If fans were cheering, I didn't hear it, all other sounds obliterated by the thunderous, roaring din of engines.

The first fifteen minutes were spectacular, crash after crash: big, side-impact wallops that sent the battered cars careening off the track, or spinning wildly out of control. Whole sides of cars were pushed in; grills caved; wheels bent back like flexing wrists; trunks popped open. A couple of the injured cars limped off to the pits. The ones that died on the track stayed there, creating dangerous obstacles.

Soon enough just five cars were left, including my father's champion, the Chevy, and my noble Datsun 510. The cars had enough space on the track that they could time the crossing at the center to avoid collision, and for several minutes there was nothing to watch but five cars running around in a figure-8. The ice had become so ravaged that all the cars slid and fishtailed, plumes of ice billowing from every wheel well.

In the bleachers I felt cold and stiff. My hot chocolate had cooled to a chalky sludge. Though I had at least three layers on, I swore I felt the icy cold of the metal bleachers burning my backside. Fingers and ears tingled. I pulled snug the scarf around my lower face.

My father took another nip from his flask, followed by a low, satisfactory purr. He asked what I thought of the race so far.

"I want to go home."

"Oh, come on, they're just getting into the stretch. Here's where the strategy and the timing come in. They'll ride it out until the final few laps, and then it'll be a blood bath. You'll see!"

Strategy? Even I, a twelve-year-old, could see that the strategy consisted of little more than eyeing your opponent and calculating whether it was safest to accelerate or decelerate through the lone dangerous spot on the course. Having made it this far, taking a few shots, the drivers were playing it safe. I thought to myself that I had never seen a spectacle so stupid as a half-dozen jalopies parading nose-to-tail like a herd of rats. The only thing more stupid were the morons watching.

This went on for dozens of laps, a freezing eternity. Those who imagine hell must be a cold place, I can tell you: it is Malosky Stadium on a winter's day, ninety laps into a one-hundred lap demolition ice race.

In the final laps my father's prediction rang true and the cars began to angle in on each other. A big Ford plowed into the Plymouth Duster, sending it into a fantastic tailspin. The Duster smashed into a snow bank, sending up a tremendous cloud of snow and hay bales—surely the most spectacular crash of the afternoon. It energized what was left of the crowd, which began to cheer and whoop. Then the Ford's steering gave out, and we watched as the car helplessly plowed into a Buick that had died in lap two, and that's all she wrote. Three cars left: my father's Chevy, my Datsun, and a baby blue '63 Mercury Meteor that had somehow escaped the fray.

The Mercury had been saving it up for the home stretch. He began driving like a maniac, weaving all over the track in an effort to collide with the Datsun, but the 510 was having none of it. Nimble of foot where the Mercury could only lumber oafishly, the Datsun and the Mercury played a game of cat-and-mouse, leaving the Chevy out of the picture—or so you might think. The

Mercury was so intent on crushing the Datsun he failed to see the Chevy timing his crossing at the center of the track. The Chevy caught the Mercury on the front quarter panel, absolutely crushing it. It hit so hard that the two cars actually did a 360, locked in a strange, slow dance, spinning into one of the open spaces inside the track. This left my wee Datsun as the sole survivor. It sailed across the finish line uncontested, the driver waving as he took a victory lap.

My father was on his feet, hooting. The fact that I'd picked the winner delighted him. "Wish we had real money on it," he bellowed. "You'd have come in twenty-to-one. God damn, Jackie, you picked it!"

There was a brief presentation to the winner, one Charles "Chip" Mientkiewicz, an ore handler from Superior, Wisconsin. Fewer than a dozen fans were left in the stands, frozen out of their skulls. The brief burst of excitement at race's end quickly dissipated, like my breath in the frigid air. I pulled on my father's coat sleeve, eager to drag him out of the stadium. He was slow to follow, recounting every detail of the race's final minutes, relishing the crushing blows and spinning crashes.

"This was fun, wasn't it, Jackie?"

"I'm cold."

"Oh, well, sure you're cold," he snarled. "Hell, I'm cold. But this is something special. This is something you only get *when* you're cold."

Whatever. We had a long walk to a frozen car, a car that I already knew would fail to warm me as we puttered home on icy roads. I calculated the minutes until I would step into the back hallway of our house and begin peeling the layers off. A warm bath, a cup of my mother's hot chocolate, perhaps a blanket on the couch—these were the things I wanted.

We got into the Pontiac. My father drained the last sip from his flask then tossed it into the glove box. He inserted the key into the ignition. The engine made a gutteral, churning sound. He tried again. A staccato ticking was all we heard.

Dad sat back and sighed, hands gripping the steering wheel. In the stillness I heard him breathing, a slow, contemplative drawing of air through his nostrils.

"Dead battery," he said.

He tried the key a couple more times.

"We'll have to walk."

"Walk?" This had to be a joke.

"At least back to Woodland Avenue, where we might catch a bus. But at that point what's the difference. Come on, it's only a mile or so."

The news shocked me into silence. I literally couldn't even think of a protest to bleat, not that it would've done any good. I sat in the car, staring stupidly at the chrome button on the glove box, until my father tapped on the glass, motioning for me to get out.

We began walking. I asked how a car battery could simply die like that, since it'd started earlier.

"Sure, with the car plugged into the block heater. She sits for a couple of hours in this cold with a half-dead battery? Different story." The laugh that followed wasn't comforting.

In milder weather the walk would have been pleasant. But on a frigidly cold February afternoon, with the light already fading into gloomy dusk, walking on icy sidewalks into a light, northerly breeze that was enough to keep your eyes watering, nose running, and exposed flesh tingling with the promise of frostbite, it was slow going. I wore so many layers I looked like the Michelin man waddling along the sidewalk. With his long loping gait my father kept bounding ahead of me. He'd stop at a corner and wait, chiding me for my slowness. I said nothing, cursing his stupid idea to go to an ice race, cursing the stupid car battery, cursing the stupid north wind. Clearly I had no good luck at all. My father was wrong on that count.

At the corner of St. Marie and Woodland stood Erikson's Swedish Restaurant. My father suggested we step inside for a bracer. It sounded good to me. At that moment I would have walked into a meat locker if I thought it would be warmer than that street corner.

With its dark timber tones and casement windows decorated with diamond muntins, Erikson's was a local favorite, one of the best Swedish restaurants in town. (Yes, there's more than one in Duluth.) In the front was a narrow dining room, just a dozen tables or so, covered in white linen tablecloths. A plump, gray-haired woman sat at one table, folding napkins. She smiled and told us the restaurant didn't open until five, but the lounge was open.

"The lounge it is," my father said.

Said lounge was a cozy, wood-paneled room with a few small tables and an oaken bar, behind which stood a man in a crisp white shirt, stacking glasses. My father made a great show of removing his hat and gloves, commenting on the cold and explaining that we'd just walked from Malosky Stadium after his car battery had died.

"We need a warm-up," he concluded.

The bartender nodded. "You're in the right place."

My father ordered a double Bourbon on the rocks. I asked for a cup of hot tea. We sat at a little table in the corner near a window. Dusk was coming on. The cars on Woodland Avenue all had their lights on. My tea came—a little pot of hot water, an empty coffee cup, and a bag of Constant Comment. As

I poured the hot water into the cup, steam billowed up, gently brushing my face. It was the best feeling I'd had all day. I sank the tea bag in and wrapped my hand around the mug.

"That'll warm you right up," my father said. "Not too far to go now."

"I wish Mom had a car."

"Wouldn't that be nice," he said, sipping his drink. "Not that she'd want to pick me up."

"Why do you guys fight so much?"

My father turned his glass around in a circle on the tabletop. "Let's just say there's been a misunderstanding."

"About what?"

"Everything."

I sank back in my seat. It was the old snow job again: when your parents didn't want to confide in you, they spoke in this vague, abstract way. I hated it.

"You hungry?" my father asked. "They have good fish."

I looked at his glass, already half-empty. "I want to go home."

"What's your rush? Don't you remember it's cold out there?"

He handed me a menu and told me to look it over. It was Swedish, all right: meatballs, potato pancakes, dumplings, pork sausage, and pickled herring.

I handed the menu back to him.

"I'm looking at that herring," he said.

He stepped up to the bar and ordered a plate of herring and a tumbler of Swedish beer. Then he and the bartender got talking about the Winter Olympics. How about the U.S. hockey team? My father had a good feeling. After tying Sweden 2-2, we'd shocked the sports world by whipping Czechoslovakia 7-3. Victories over Norway, Romania, and West Germany quickly followed. Somehow the underdog Americans had made it to the medal round and would face Russia next Friday in Lake Placid.

"They have no chance," the bartender groused.

"Don't be so sure," Dad said. "Czechoslovakia was everyone's favorite for the silver."

The bartender leaned forward, two hands on the bar. "You're talking about the Russian national team. They're bred for one thing. Losing is not an option."

Such talk sounded disturbingly familiar. Whether it was ice hockey or the space race, the Russians were determined to beat the West. Next Friday would be a blood bath, no question.

I finished my tea and was definitely feeling warmer. But I felt tired and cranky, too. This day, which had held so much promise, had turned into a disaster. It was the kind of thing my father could laugh at. He was laughing now, leaning an elbow on the bar, chatting freely with his new pal, enjoying himself despite his worries. This was the father I was used to seeing when I was out with him, when he was at work or at a party: a man who shook off his troubles around strangers but wore them like a hair shirt around our house. For so long I had simply accepted this—that my father acted one way with strangers or friends, and another with my mother and me. But on that afternoon darker, more resentful feelings took hold. I wondered, Why do families endure each other? It seemed illogical, improbable, absurd.

A plump, gray-haired waitress came with a plate of herring for my father.

He took one bite, then gestured to the heavens in awe. "Jackie, you'll want some of this."

I shook my head.

"Suit yourself." He called for more liquor.

I stood, intent on visiting the men's room. I took my coat from the chair. When I'd finished I stood in the hallway, mid-way between the bar and the dining room. I heard my father laughing. I hesitated, studying a small accumulation of dust in the corner of a windowsill, some small, hard-to-clean spot that had been overlooked. I turned and walked through the dining room and out onto Woodland Avenue.

I arrived home to find my mother sick with worry. We hadn't called, she had no idea where we were, she didn't know what had happened to us. I explained the saga of the car, our long walk to Erikson's, and concluded by simply stating that I'd chosen to leave and my father had chosen to stay.

Surprisingly, she didn't ask why. That had been my major worry on the short walk home—how to explain what I'd done. Temperatures were well below freezing, it was dark out. If anything had happened I might have frozen to death in a snowbank and not been discovered until April. But my mother didn't question my motives. I understood, in the way that a son can intuit something from his mother, that perhaps I'd done the right thing.

I had my dinner and bath, watched an hour of television, and climbed into bed without my father so much as showing the toe of his boot in the house. My mother sat in a chair in the living room, her nose buried in Fielding's *Tom Jones*, which she was reading for her literature class. She appeared calm and composed, which impressed me, though I noticed a bevy of balled-up tissues on the floor at her feet.

I'd been in bed for thirty minutes when Dad arrived. The shouting began immediately. He was drunk, his voice booming like a detuned kettle drum. Mom shot staccato accusations back at him, not pausing to hear his response. In high dudgeon, she was merciless, sharp, and hard. Like a soldier running for cover under fire, my father retreated into the basement to sleep it off on the couch.

The calm that followed was quickly broken by the sound of my mother's sobbing, her tears unbottled now, slowly filling the living room. A sea of tears destined to drown her, him, and me.

Though Dad and I had planned to watch the U.S. hockey match together he was nowhere to be found on Friday. He did not come home from work. He was not present at the dinner table. Mom and I ate in silence, one empty plate across from us.

I watched the game alone in the basement of our house. My father's good feeling proved correct: the Americans beat the Russians 4-3, the famous "Miracle on Ice," stunning the world. I was as thrilled and as exuberant as anyone—it really was an impossible dream come true, and a moment I will never forget—but when I look back on it now I also remember a sadness that my father was not there to share the moment, despite making plans. That his absence that evening was both unexpected and unexplained only made my mother's worry and my grief stronger.

But I thought I understood it. Dad and I had hardly spoken since I'd left him at Erikson's. My proud defiance quickly gave way to sickening worry that I'd angered him, and he resented me.

Dad was with me the following Sunday morning when the Americans beat Finland to claim the gold medal. I'm not sure he saw much of the game. He lay on the couch, a wet towel draped across his brow, sipping water and cursing all forms of light. My shout of glee when the clock ticked down to zero in the third period was met with a bark to pipe down.

2

In March Mr. Baird left school to undergo treatment for lung cancer. Ms. Barbara Poindexter was appointed our substitute for the remainder of sixth grade. Poindexter was short, not much taller than my best friend John Skoglund, who was pushing five-two that year. She wore turtlenecks under thick wool sweaters, hand-dyed stockings beneath beaded skirts, and long ropes of beads around her neck. Her hair hung in a ponytail, brushing her waistline. I don't recall her ever wearing pants. She wore long dresses or skirts, even on cold days. She'd recently returned from Africa, she informed us, where she'd served in the Peace Corps. Did anyone know where Kenya was on the map?

A half-dozen hands shot up, including John's. When Poindexter called on him he pointed vaguely in the direction of central Asia.

"No, sorry, wrong continent. *This* is Africa," she said, tapping the vinyl map with her rubber-tipped stick.

John shrugged. "Miss, your sweater's dirty."

The room fell silent, waiting for her response. John was right, sort of. Her sweater bore dingy gray streaks that resembled ground-in dirt, or perhaps the ash from a fire. Poindexter frowned and cleared her throat. She explained that the sweater wasn't dirty, it was made from unbleached wool, made by a sheep farmer in Oregon who'd been a conscientious objector during the Vietnam War. Did we children understand what it meant to stand up for a principle at any cost? That's one definition of patriotism. This sheep farmer could recite the preamble of the U.S. Constitution from memory and make it sound like a poem.

Then she asked us who founded America.

"Miss," said Jill McGilligan, "we usually do math in the mornings and history after lunch."

"You'll take a bit of history right now, won't you," Poindexter shot back.

That's when we knew we were in for something different. Baird, that lovable old walrus, had been easily swayed off topic. He loved a joke—usually concerning Ole the Big Swede or Finn Finsky from Finland—often giving over large parts of a lesson to sharing them. But he stuck to the schedule with unerring predictability.

"And, please," she continued, "it's Ms. Poindexter, not Miss."

"What's the difference?"

That was me. I asked one earnest question a day. I still do. But only one.

Poindexter informed us that "Miss" referred to a single woman, unmarried, but there was an implied expectation, culturally, that marriage would or should follow. "Mrs." denoted marriage and, as she put it, conformity to normative social standards. "Ms." was used regardless of marital status. It conveyed a sense of independence and autonomy. "And that is Ms. Poindexter. Everyone, say it with me: *mizz, mizz, mizz.*"

We droned along with her, an army of drunken bees.

Then it was onto Chapter Fifteen in our history book, *The Founding of America*. Poindexter opened her text, gave it a cursory glance, and muttered, "Yes, yes, I see." She shut the book, dropped it with a loud *thunk* on her desk, and began walking back and forth at the front of the room, hands behind her back, asking questions. Who, in fact, did found America? The answer came quickly: It was the Pilgrims, who landed at Plymouth in 1620. Why did they come? To flee religious persecution—the Church of England, blah blah blah. She seemed impressed with our quick, accurate answers. (We could thank Jill McGilligan and her brown-nosing posse in row one for that dog-and-pony show.) Then she asked us if we'd heard of the Jamestown Colony. No, we hadn't studied that.

Actually, I had. I'd read ahead in the book. In fact, I'd read the entire book. History was a topic that grabbed me early. But I wasn't about to say anything and risk being seen as a suck-up.

"One might argue," she said, "that America was not founded on principles of religious freedom, or at least not *exclusively* on those principles. Jamestown was a speculative business enterprise—the long arm of capitalism, as it were."

Kids were flipping madly through their books, trying to find the passage to which she was referring. No such luck. They were used to studying history with Old Baird, which meant reading along with him, word-for-word. You could nap while he droned on—he didn't give a rat's ass—and catch up on your reading at home. Not so with Ms. Poindexter. She was young and sort of vaguely pretty, I'd decided. To be sure, she was exotic, at least for Duluth in 1980. And she was all substance. She paced back and forth, one slender hand jabbing at the air as she told us that the founding of America could be explained in a number of ways. There were, of course, the native Americans who lived here first and who were brutally killed off by violence and disease, their land stolen by invading Europeans.

"Never forget," she said, "America is an empire of blood."

She looked slowly around the room. Her gaze seemed accusatory, provocative, daring any of us to debate.

"For better or worse," she continued, "the Europeans conquered the natives. But which Europeans landed first?"

"Columbus," someone chirped.

"Never set foot in North America," Poindexter replied. "Most likely it was Leif Erickson, circa 1000 A.D. Sod huts and salted cod—not much of a legacy, I'm afraid. Not enough pizazz." Columbus, landing a half-century later, got the credit because he was a better salesman, bringing back captive natives, parrots, and gold. It stirred people up, made them want to travel. But it was merely showbiz. "In truth, Columbus was a lousy businessman and a terrible leader. His own shipmates sent him back to España in chains. He died a failure."

"What?" I blurted out. I couldn't help it. It felt like the back of my head had exploded. This *definitely* wasn't in the book.

Poindexter pressed on. The first permanent European settlement was established in St. Augustine, Florida by the Spaniard Pedro Menéndez de Avilés, 1565. This only after he'd brutally massacred his French rivals in South Carolina.

"But the French and the Spanish—alas, mere dabblers," she continued, flicking her hand. "When America tells itself its history we start with the exodus from England to—*quelle surprise!*—*New* England. And so we begin, somewhat arbitrarily, one might argue, with the Pilgrims in 1620. If, that is, you want to believe that this country actually values religious diversity. A debatable point, but that is a discussion for another day. Starting with Jamestown Island in 1607 we have a different story all together: we see that the Yankee dollar has always, from the first minute, been the driving impetus behind all things 'American.'

"My point today, dear charges, is that our story begins not with the first Europeans to visit America, but with the first English settlers to establish a permanent settlement, the first to convene a democratic assembly in North America, and all the rest. As Americans we have selected these men—and they were all men in Jamestown, initially—as our forefathers. But another version of the story might be constructed. There is always a history other than the history you receive, other ways of telling the story. I want you to remember that."

The lunch bell rang as if on cue. We were out of there like bullets from a gun. Our first mission, always, was to race down the hallway making as much noise as possible and get in the hot lunch line to receive our plate of slop, then claim the seats that we boys always claimed over in the corner by the big windows. All that while I found myself thinking over what Poindexter had told us. I wasn't entirely sure what she was going on about. I only knew that, unlike most of the teachers I'd encountered up to that point, she knew something that wasn't in our books. What she taught came from another place. I'd never heard any teacher speak like that. It electrified me.

For John it was another matter entirely.

"Jesus Fucking Mary," he spat, "Poindexter is horrible! If I have to sit through three months of that I'll puke."

To resist and sidetrack Poindexter became John's holy mission that spring, giving shape and focus to his otherwise ungrounded classroom existence. If Poindexter asked for quiet, he whispered conspiratorially in our corner. If we were assigned reading or writing exercises, he made paper airplanes. During art, he deliberately mixed up paint jars, scattered crayons, or folded paper incorrectly. When it was music time and we were asked to produce our recorders to play "All Ye Bonny Gentlemen" or "Yankee Doodle," John deliberately played off key, or simply produced farting noises, sending a peal of laughter around the room.

I tolerated this behavior in my friend but I did not join him. I no longer followed John blindly. In fact I'd spent most of sixth grade working hard to earn good grades. Though I hadn't announced it to anyone, I wanted to see if I could get a straight-A report card. I had a lot of work to do, especially in math, but I wanted to see how close I could get. I knew Poindexter could help me.

I was in my bedroom looking through a book on Soviet air power when my father stepped through the door, waving a yellow baseball flyer we'd received in the mail. "Did you see this, Jackie? Twelve-year-olds can try out for the Junior Leagues this year. I'll bet Skoglund is going up. How about you?"

My father was a handsome man, tall and lean with a shock of black hair he kept slicked back against his head with pomade. He wore sport coats and dress trousers, and he looked good in them. He was straight home from work: another day of pushing shiny, foreign kitchenware at bored housewives with money to burn. He once told me that his stuff was so classy no one north of Minneapolis had any business buying it. He didn't mention if a guy from Hibbing had any business selling it.

I slowly turned a page in my book, revealing the awesome MIG-23 Wolfcat, a long-range fighter-bomber that could deliver a 15,000 pound payload. Enough to wipe out a couple of blocks in our neighborhood if the Russians decided to bomb civilians, which I did not doubt.

"I guess so," I said.

My father frowned. "You're not excited."

I locked my most serious, steady gaze on him, the gaze of a fighter pilot trained in on his kill. "I said I'll do it."

"Then you have a few weeks to get in shape." He flicked the paper with his finger tip. "That's if you really want it."

He placed the flyer beside me on the bed and left my room. I brushed it onto the floor with the back of my arm.

The winter before, at my father's urging, I had tried to jump ahead in ice hockey, following John into the Bantam league. We'd been together all the way from Ice Mice through Squirts to Pee Wee. We'd come to think of ourselves as a kind of unstoppable duo, securing our team on the rink and taking care of business. John was quick and light on his skates, a talented puck handler. He'd been encouraged to make the leap up to Bantams and had done so with relative ease. Not so for poor old Jackie Rose. I was a hard-skating, hard-hitting defenseman. I had grit and ambition, but I was no John Skoglund. My sprints from behind the net out to center ice were slow, and I never did have much of a slap shot. Plus I was short for my age. Those kids in Bantam towered over me, pushing me around like a cat toy. The coaches were kind in their assessment, assuring me that next year, when I was eligible, they'd be glad to have me. Meanwhile, it was back to Pee Wee.

I had a respectable season. My teammate Jerry Gustafson and I led Glen Avon to the semi-finals of the city tournament. Although we lost to the Hermantown Hornets, it was the greatest accomplishment of my hockey career thus far. John was there to cheer us on and console us after our loss, and of course I appreciated that, though seeing him in his orange-and-black Bantam team jacket stung a little. What stung more was the unspoken fact that, in failing to keep pace with John, I'd disappointed my father.

In his day Dad been no chump on the ice, playing four years of high school varsity up in Hibbing. He set a scoring record his junior year, a record unmatched for a decade. The saga of the mighty Hibbing Rangers and their trip to the state tourney in his senior year was the stuff of legend in our house. The Rangers had been underdogs, written off by everyone. They fought their way through every round, taking advantage of power plays, scoring last-minute goals. They clinched the final in double-overtime, upsetting the reigning champs and getting their faces on the cover of every newspaper in the state. My father could describe every minute of that season in excruciating detail. And, after a couple of beers, he often did.

But his hockey career ended there, at age eighteen. Dad had no plans for college. No one in his family had ever been. His place, he was told, was

on his father's dairy farm outside Hibbing, a role he grudgingly filled. His pals trucked off to Madison, Minneapolis, and Marquette on scholarships. Watching them leave, one after the other, had been a bitter pill.

Dad put in a few years on the farm—long enough, as he put it, to see the writing on the wall. Small, single-family dairies were dying out. He urged his family to sell. My grandfather had other ideas, none of which involved retirement. Things turned nasty, just how nasty my father would never say (he *never* discussed his relationship with his father), but we all know what he did: he abruptly walked off the farm, irrevocably estranging himself from his family.

Dad enlisted in the Air Force where he trained as a jet engine mechanic. He served four years overseas, one tour in Vietnam followed by lighter assignments in Japan and West Germany. He took his discharge in Duluth, met and married my mother, and landed a civilian job at the air base with the 148th Fighter Group, servicing the F-89 Scorpion and the F-101 Voodoo. In '76 the fighter wing was reassigned to tactical reconnaissance, the first of a string of changes that would eventually lead to the closing of the base. Civilian contractors were laid off in droves, my father among them.

There was talk of following the work, haunting bases out in California or Alaska. But none of that was a sure thing, and my father proved a cautious man. A buddy hooked him up with the job at Weimann & Brothers, a downtown department store, where he learned the virtues of collectible plate ware, high-end German cutlery, and all the rest. He made a decent living though he had no special affection for the work.

3

That spring the sixth-grade girls formed one gang and the boys another. We took turns launching raids on one another, which usually involved isolating some member of the opposing side, kidnapping her, and holding her for ransom. One afternoon, as I was sneaking around the back of the ice warming shed, I was surprised by three girls, led by Marta Haugen. They immediately took me prisoner, a girl holding me by each arm, pressing me back against the wooden wall of the shed, alongside the small propane tank, out of sight from the playground. It was damp and shadowy there. I studied a small patch of dirty snow that hadn't yet melted between the propane tank and the shed wall.

Marta had been held back a grade, the lone teenager in our sixth grade classroom. She had full red lips and round cheeks. Standing before me like a Norse warrior, her long blonde hair hanging in braided ropes over each shoulder, she declared that I would be held for ransom, as the boys had captured Lauren Polk. Marta immediately dispatched my two guards as messengers to enact the transfer. She would watch me herself. Two girls darted off to deliver the demand and I was left alone behind the warming shed with Marta.

She stepped toward me, hands on hips, a smile in one corner of her mouth. "Now that I've got you, I might torture you a little." She stepped closer.

Gooseflesh prickled across my arms. This was part of her pirate game, though the look in her eye wasn't exactly confrontational. I pushed myself forward, off the wall. If I bolted now I had a shot at escape.

"Don't move," she whispered. "Put your hands behind your back."

The power of a soft word, spoken privately by a girl to a boy, is unequaled by the loudest of tyrants. I did as I was told. I felt a querulous trembling in my gut. My breath quickened. Marta stepped even closer, standing just inches from me, eyes half-closed. I didn't know what to make of it. I lowered my gaze, studying the maroon and navy stripes across the white field of her shirt. I was surprised to see her abdomen drawing in and out as rapidly as mine. I heard her breath, quick and light.

"Are you ready?"

I looked up. "For what?"

She pressed her full, warm lips against mine, holding them there for a moment, motionless. I couldn't think, didn't know what was happening. I certainly couldn't move.

She stepped back. "Now you're mine, Jackie Rose."

Her lips tasted of grape bubble gum, slightly sticky and sweet. I'd never been kissed before, not like that. And if I wasn't sure I liked it, I certainly didn't dislike it.

From behind Marta a sharp voice called out, "Let him go."

John Skoglund stood before us, arms folded across his chest, head cocked with panache. I knew where he'd lifted that look. It was Danny Zuko in *Grease*. We'd seen the movie three times last summer, drooling over Olivia Newton John in those skin-tight leather pants.

In the coolest voice imaginable, John repeated his demand.

Marta planted a hand on one hip. "What if I don't?"

Oh, I loved her then.

John lifted an eyebrow. He was not used to being refused, especially by a girl. "It's all right," I told John. "It's not so bad."

Frowning, John asked what we'd been doing.

"Wouldn't you like to know," Marta said.

John took a step forward. I was unsure what would happen next, but we were all saved a moment later by the arrival of a posse of boys escorting Lauren Polk, followed by a troop of girls. After a brief declaration of terms Lauren and I were exchanged. I was free to go.

I stepped forward into sunlight. Marta put a hand on my forearm. She whispered in my ear, "Don't forget, you're mine."

Her voice lingered in my ear for the duration of recess. It was still there when the bell rang, calling us back to our studies. And it is there now.

My mother, a tall, wispy Swede, never carried an ounce of fat. In fact, in later years she would become so gaunt I'd worry she might blow away. For most of my childhood she'd been a stay-at-home mom. She cooked enormous meals for me and my father—pot roasts, pork tenderloins, and my favorite, Swedish meatballs—yet she only picked at her food. Her attention to me had always been complete. Over the years she'd served as Den Mother for Cub Scouts, a lead parent for my hockey squad, or a volunteer librarian at Washburn Elementary. Much to my chagrin she even taught Sunday school at Glen Avon Presbyterian, which of course made my attendance mandatory.

That spring my mother did something unexpected. She enrolled in two courses at the University of Minnesota, Duluth, studying western history and British literature. This disrupted the family routine in minor ways. On Tuesdays and Thursday afternoons I came home to an empty house. While we still ate dinner together as a family, the offerings became less elaborate. Simpler and faster. After dinner Mom did not sit in the living room with me watching *The Six Million Dollar Man* or *Mork & Mindy*. She had her nose buried in *Middlemarch*, or was drafting an essay on the Roman occupation of Gaul.

Her decision to go to school was one of many things my parents fought about. Dad said she was wasting her time and his money, taking those fool classes over at the college. This made her cry. She called him sharp names, things I'd never heard her say. She said he resented her, felt threatened by her. Just because he was unhappy with his position didn't mean she had to sit tight in hers.

When she said things like that my father went berserk, launching a new round of shouting, the mad crescendo billowing up until he declared he'd had enough. He abruptly left my mother mid-sentence and stomped down the back stairs into his half-finished basement, where he sat in his green armchair talking back to his TV shows. Some nights my mother followed him down there. Like warring giants, they rumbled in the catacombs. Other nights she stood at the lip of the stairwell, shouting that she hadn't married a chauvinist pig, so why had he turned into one?

She might throw something after him. We lost a lot of glassware that year.

When it got really bad I ran upstairs to my room, shut the door, and put a 45 on my tiny all-in-one turntable. I had quite a collection, singles being nearly the only thing I spent my money on. I loved best those songs that told a story, creating a little world in my head, some place I could disappear into. Al Stewart's "Year of the Cat," or "Sultans of Swing" by Dire Straits. But of all the songs in my collection, none struck deeper than Gerry Rafferty's "Baker Street." It seemed mysterious and knowing, a message from foreign shores; it spoke of a world just out of reach. A saxophone rose from the swell of noise, standing somehow above it all, triumphant and alive. I saw London streets filled with double-decker busses and black taxis and people in gabardine trench coats pulled tight against the damp mist. I wanted to go there, to walk those streets, and to know.

By sixth grade I had cultivated an intense dislike for all forms of math. I still hadn't memorized my multiplication tables. When Old Baird was around

I taped a hand-written times table to my desktop. Why memorize? Poindexter shaved the tables off my desk as quickly as I put them on.

One afternoon Poindexter sent our class across the hall to Mr. Zoller's room to watch a film. She asked me to stay behind to work on math. We sat beside one another at her big oak desk with a sheet of problems spread out before us, converting fractions to a decimal. I was supposed to walk her through each problem. It was a lot of work. I was slow and needed copious amounts of scratch paper. I understood I was lagging behind my peers. Even John Skoglund could whip through a math worksheet like walking down the street. Sitting there with Poindexter leaning over my shoulder, asking me to explain each step of the problem, made me doubly anxious.

From across the hall I heard a swell of laughter and calls from the louder boys. My heart ached for the lost hour of television, for all the joking and poking and shenanigans going on there in the dark.

"Jackie." I heard my name, breaking my reverie. "Jackie, hello."

I sat up with a start and returned my attention to the math problem. I'd left off somewhere in the middle. It seemed interminable, this work. On Poindexter's desk was a photo of soldier standing stiffly at attention, an American flag in the background. I asked if that was her husband.

"No, that's my brother. He served with the marines in Vietnam. He died there, very near the end of the war."

"He had a lot of medals," I said. "Was he a hero?"

She picked up the photo and studied it. "I suppose. He did as he was told and he did it well. That's one definition of duty."

"Like being in school."

"Not exactly."

She sat back in her chair, still staring at the photo. "It's important to listen to your teachers and to follow the rules, but the true purpose of an education is not to follow orders blindly. It's to learn to think for yourself, to grow up with an active, critical mind. To be informed about things." She set the photo down. "There might be a day when someone—your government, perhaps—will order you to do something, like fight in a war. You might decide to do it, or you might not."

I thought about that for a second.

"You're saying your brother shouldn't have fought in that war."

"It wasn't my choice to make."

"But what if it had been?"

She tapped a pencil against the back of her hand. "I would have refused."

"Why?"

"Because I'm a pacifist."

"Somebody who won't fight."

"Someone who *chooses* not to fight because she believes there are other, better ways of settling disputes. Non-violence."

I doodled in the corner of my worksheet, thinking about a book I'd read by one of the pilots of *Enola Gay*. Dropping the A-bombs quickened the war's end, he'd argued, saving American lives. A terrible choice to make, but the right one.

"Aren't some wars justified?" I asked.

Poindexter lifted her chin. "Perhaps, but not the Vietnam War. It was a mistake. It deeply dishonored our country. It pains me, knowing my brother had a hand in that." She was quiet for a moment, then added, "He was so brash. I often wonder if he knew we were losing the war, if he could admit that."

"The United States has never lost a war," I said, parroting my father.

A frown crinkled the corner of her mouth. "I don't suppose you've ever heard of the War of 1812."

But I had. Last fall I'd delivered an oral report on Andrew Jackson and the Battle of New Orleans. That war ended in a draw, I told her.

"Stalemate is hardly victory," she replied. "In war either you achieve your stated goal or you don't. Thus went the War of 1812, and thus went Vietnam."

I didn't know quite what to say to that. I wasn't sure she was right, though I couldn't see how she was wrong. It shocked me to think that the United States might have lost not one but two wars. Why wasn't this better known?

Poindexter tapped a finger on my math pages.

"It's time to return to your math problems, Mr. Rose."

I rolled my eyes, about to bleat in protest, when the bell rang. Almost instantly Mr. Zoller's door flew open and a stream of children poured forth. Poindexter released me and I quickly joined my friends. I didn't tell anyone about my extra homework, let alone Poindexter's brother, or what we'd talked about. I kept those secrets to myself.

On the first Wednesday of every month the air raid sirens sounded at noon, a distant, mournful wail, melancholy and forlorn. In class we were instructed to crawl under our desks, hunched into a ball, hands clasped behind our heads. Our teachers called this a Civil Defense drill, but I knew better. The sirens were for one thing and one thing only: to warn of a Soviet missile attack.

It was the Cold War. The Russians were unsentimental, vicious drunkards, intent on flattening the United States. They had no God, no correct sense of history, no compunction about killing millions of innocent civilians. Their tanks would grind over the bones of our children; they drank aftershave when their vodka gave out; they could survive on nothing but potatoes. Having been double-crossed in World War Two, they trusted no one and ignored all pleas for mercy. The only sensible option was to nuke them before they nuked us.

Duluth was ninth on the Russian list of U.S. cities to annihilate, or so I'd heard. It made sense to me. We had one of North America's largest inland ports. We had an air base with a wing of military fighter jets. We mattered, we rated with the Soviets. I carried this fact around in my twelve-year-old head, drunk with a sense of importance. Weren't Soviet spies lurking in the back streets of our city? Didn't satellite cameras record our every movement? Surely a Russian submarine hovered in the icy waters of Lake Superior, waiting for the signal to torpedo an outgoing ore boat and then launch a ballistic missile. Like some junior doomsday philosopher, I walked the hills of Duluth assuming our days were numbered. And life seemed richer: hearing the Beatles sing "Strawberry Fields Forever" on my tiny turntable brought me into rhapsody, for this might be the last time that beautiful song would be played for the free and the brave. What a shame to lose such art to those mad, insatiable Russian interlopers.

In my daydreams I survived whatever attack befell us. I saw myself standing alone at the foot of Enger Tower, overlooking West Duluth, the Bong Memorial Bridge, and the ore docks stretching out along the southwest shore of the lake. I dreamed of nuclear winter, ash falling from the sky on a bleak gray dawn. I saw a young boy wandering empty streets, scrounging for food, turning his eye away from the shadows of the dead, those ghoulish murals burned into the walls of buildings. The boy wanders among empty houses, scouring the malls and air raid shelters, searching for fellow survivors. His loneliness is both a curse and a solemn responsibility, for he has taken it upon himself to compose a history of what was lost, a record of his time and place, an attempt to give shape and form to something chaotic and disastrous, what would otherwise be only a legacy of pain and loss. This is his testament.

Marta was sending me notes. Did I love her? Was I thinking of her? Was I her one and only? Always, there were two boxes at the bottom: YES/NO. I was to check the appropriate answer and return the message via her courier, Carrie Walczak. I dutifully marked YES and returned the notes. Then I waited. I didn't know what else to do.

It wasn't that I disliked Marta. Quite the opposite. I found her strangely powerful. She excited me in ways I couldn't understand. Marta knew something I did not, and this intimidated me. Being intellectually curious but emotionally timid, I naturally shied away from her.

On Friday our class went to the library. We were required to find a book for our next book report. I found one on the U.S.-Soviet space race and retired to my favorite corner, a sunny little nook in the back with some chairs and couches. I marveled over grainy black-and-white shots of Soyuz 1 and 2, and the brave little dog Laika, first animal to orbit the earth.

Marta dropped into the chair beside me and asked what I was reading. I explained how the Soviet triumph with Sputnik was a cold blow to the Americans, who were further humiliated when their attempt to launch the Vanguard rocket failed. I showed her a picture of the explosion, a tremendous orange fireball on the launch pad. "Everything was destroyed," I concluded, my throat tight with awe for the sheer spectacle of the devastation.

"Huh."

I asked what she was reading. She held up a book on castles. On the cover, the famous Neuschwanstein, with its crenellated white towers, perched on a rock in Bavaria.

"I want to live there," she announced.

I told her my dad had seen it. He'd been stationed at an air base in West Germany for two years and had travelled all over the region. He'd also been to Windsor castle in England and Versailles in France. He had slides of everything, a seemingly endless amount of them.

"Would you live in a castle with me?" Marta asked.

"Sure."

"You'd have to marry me. That way we could be king and queen."

Leaning forward, she ran a fingertip along the top edge of my book. I studied the tip of that finger, trimmed down close to the nub.

"Do you want to go with me?"

"To Bavaria? I said okay."

She frowned. "No, do you want to 'go' with me."

I sat back, flabbergasted. Why hadn't I seen this coming? All of my male friends were "going" with some girl, or talking about asking a girl to go with them. This was all the rage in sixth grade. I wasn't sure where the idea had come from, or exactly what it meant. I only knew that if you were going with somebody word spread and it was universally praised. I'd watched, mystified, as my pals paired off, one after the other. John Skoglund had been among the first, announcing as far back as last Thanksgiving that he was going with Carrie Walczak. I'd been encouraged to pick somebody out, but I didn't see the point. The boys still sat at their lunch table, the girls at theirs, and at recess we still played our silly hostage games and acted as if we couldn't stand one another.

Marta cocked her head to one side, impossibly sweet. "Well?"

I closed the book in my lap. She demanded an answer, the one thing my brain could not produce at that moment. Yet who was I to refuse this future queen? I said yes.

A big smile brightened her face. "I knew it!"

She pecked me quickly on the cheek, then darted off around a corner, vanishing as quickly as she'd appeared, leaving me more confused than ever.

4

On Saturday my father took John Skoglund and me to the batting cages near the Miller Hill Mall. This was a new joint, a combination mini-golf/pizza parlor/pinball arcade and, in warmer weather, an outdoor batting cage. As it was a chilly March morning—snow was still piled up in the back corners of the parking lots—we had the joint to ourselves. My father put a five-dollar bill into the change machine and got a small mountain of quarters. Then he pointed to the cage and told me to get in there.

I have always liked a batting cage. It is a place designed to minimize distractions, to eliminate variables. Each pitch comes at a predictable interval, identical in execution, an endless procession of opportunity. This allows you to focus on your swing, to fine tune all the mechanical parts: your stance, that crucial step forward, how you roll your wrists as you bring the bat around, your follow-through. There is the slight jolt in your arms as the bat makes contact, the *tink* of metal meeting plastic, and then the yellow orb sails off into the netting, or bounces wildly on the concrete floor, rolling into a drain, eventually reappearing from the mouth of the machine. In the cage there are no pitchers to stare down, no infielders slapping their gloves in anticipation, no outfielders haunting the back fence. The cage is all about feel. It's about process and repetition, knowing what comes next and when. It's just you, the machine, and the ball. In the cage I hit like Johnny Bench, or at least it felt that way. It was a precious illusion—one I knew, even then, that lived only within those wire walls.

The truth is I had little skill. On a real baseball diamond I swung madly, blindly, praying for contact. I couldn't pick out a pitch or direct the hit. Any sort of contact was a stroke of good luck as far as I was concerned. If I put the ball in play—any sort of play—I'd done my job. I knew that better players like John could tell a fastball from a curve; they could aim the ball to the left or right; they could choose to hit a line drive or a pop fly. Such control seemed an impenetrable mystery.

I came out of the cage to find myself peppered with advice from my father.

Choke up on the bat. Wait a half-second on that first step. Lift your chin. I sat hunched on the cold metal of the bleacher seat, my hands jammed into the pockets of my warm-up jacket, staring silently into the netting until he'd had his say.

Then it was John's turn. My father and I sat side-by-side as we watched him take the first few pitches. His swing was easy and smooth, with a natural rhythm and grace. John had a steady, sure eye. He sent ball after ball up in what would be deep flies to the nether regions of the outfield. Then he practiced line drives, shooting bullets toward second, short, and down the lines. He was a duck hunter bagging his game, a Russian sharpshooter downing his victims with cool, heartless precision.

"That kid's got something," my father said.

I grunted my assent, trying to sound non-committal, though I knew he was right.

My father stood and noisily jangled the keys in his pocket. He announced that he had an errand, a small matter of business that needed his attention. He'd be back in a little while.

"Where are you going?"

"To see a client," he said. This seemed odd. I knew where my father worked and what he did. His clients came to him, not the other way around.

He handed me another five-dollar bill and told me to buy a couple of hot dogs and some sodas when we were done.

"Just stay right here," he told me. "I'll be back lickity split."

John finished his first round in the batting cage, then came out. "How'd it look?"

I told him it looked pretty damn fine.

He lifted his chin in the direction of the parking lot. "Where's your old man going?"

I turned to see my father's plum-colored '72 Pontiac GTO making its way out of the lot and onto the trunk highway.

I shrugged my shoulders. "He says he'll be right back."

I showed John the money I'd been given and we agreed to get some chow after the next round of swings. Thirty minutes later we sat in a red vinyl booth near a window facing the parking lot.

"So are you going with Marta Haugen? I know she asked you."

I frowned. "How do you know?"

"Carrie told me."

Marta and Carrie were best friends, and of course John was going with Carrie, so that made sense. Still, I resented people knowing Marta had asked me. It added to the pressure.

"Do you think it's weird she asked me?"

"It's better if the guy asks," he said, "but it won't matter once you get to first base."

I sat up in the booth. "I already have."

John gave me a hard stare. "Bullshit."

I told him I'd kissed her behind the warming shed a few days ago, the day she captured me. "That's what started this whole thing."

He jabbed a french fry into a pot of ketchup. "Carrie would've said something."

"Carrie doesn't know." I reveled in having something, anything over John. "Marta and I agreed, it's just between us."

John wiped his mouth on a napkin, then wadded it up and tossed it at my chest. "Well done, dingleberry. There's hope for you after all."

I couldn't contain my grin. I reached over and stole a fry.

"So you've kissed her, and you're going together," John said. "Now you have to get to second base."

I looked away, studying the fry cook as he shoved burger baskets under a heat lamp. The thought of putting my hand up a girl's shirt seemed ridiculous. But if this was the next cairn I made a silent vow to reach it, if only to keep pace with John.

I asked if he'd gotten to second base with Carrie.

"Months ago."

How'd he do it, exactly?

"You just get in there." A discussion of how to unsnap a bra without looking followed, the details of which seemed preternaturally complex.

"I can't do that," I blurted out.

John sat forward. "You're not a pussy, are you?"

"Hell no."

"All right then."

I rubbed my neck, which suddenly felt stiff and tight. John had always been two steps ahead of me, whether it was girls, sports, or the birds and the bees. Two years ago I'd mentioned to him that I sometimes heard my parents making funny noises late at night in their bedroom. Giggles and whispers, sometimes a yelp or two. John had laughed and taken me to see his older brother. Chris Skoglund related in painstaking detail how a man joins together with a woman, what happens when the various parts come together, and how, nine months later, a child results.

Disgusted, I'd told them there was no way my parents would ever do such a thing. No way in hell. Women just naturally had babies. They got married and, you know, it just sort of happened. Laughing, Chris told me to ask my mother.

I marched straight home and did just that. As I delivered my impassioned speech, a smile crept across my mother's face. I demanded that she confirm I was correct. She covered her mouth with her hand and looked at me for a long moment, then knelt before me. I stepped into her arms. She held me tight and close, kissed my cheek, and told me she loved me. Then she told me those boys were correct. "They're a bit crude, and they're mean for teasing you that way, but that's about the size of it."

Flabbergasted, I ran out of the house, slamming the door behind me. I ran to Grass Hill, a small park a couple of blocks from the house, and sat alone at the top of the hill, contemplating a world that seemed hopelessly perverted. That my parents were part of it seemed preposterous; that I was a product of it, inconceivable.

Grass Hill was a favorite spot. As soon as the first big winter storm hit, we neighborhood kids clambered up it with buckets of tap water, icing down a chute on the steepest part. With a bit of crafty shovel work, we engineered a smoothly-curved jump at its base. A good run at top speed required you to hit the jump at just the right angle so you'd clear the sidewalk that ran along the base of the hill, landing on a narrow foot trail, which cut through a stand of birch and poplar. A miscalculation would either spill you onto the frozen concrete sidewalk or send you flying into the trees. These were risks well worth taking, however, for an incomparable rush of terror and glee as you soared through the air. We recorded distances and awarded points for style. There was an unofficial King of the Hill, usually one of the older boys who, with his weight and speed, could achieve Olympian distances. Any fool who had the guts to race down that ice slick and risk splitting his head open was a blood brother, one of the merry idiots who owned that hill.

Cowardice and timidity were the only banes. The unlucky soul who found himself perched at the top of the chute, unable to muster the courage to launch, was mercilessly heckled until he made that first run or got the hell out of the way. The absolute worst thing you could do would be to half-commit, bailing mid-way and thereby damaging the chute, an act of treachery repaid with a fusillade of curses and ice-packed snowballs.

Bad things did happen. Jerry Gustafson knocked himself out cold one time, flying ass-over-teakettle, cracking his head on the frozen sidewalk. (Even now, I wince: his skull sounded just like a dropped bowling ball.) There were broken fingers, split lips, and twisted ankles. More than one kid caught hell for busting up his sled—they can only take so much punishment. Occasionally a worried parent trudged up the hill to lecture us on the dangers, ordering his unlucky son or daughter home, but these were at best temporary deterrents. Winter is not a time to be holed up in the house staring out a window. When the snow falls kids don their suits, boots, caps and mittens; they grab their skates, their skis, their snow shoes and toboggans and they race outside.

Grass Hill was a proving ground where I learned to conquer fear, performing some minor bit of craziness for the enjoyment of my peers. Few things in childhood pleased me more. There, I had feelings I now understand to be rare: that of having risked mightily, of having given all. In reward I enjoyed the fraternity of like-minded fools. I might limp home with frozen hands and a bruised backside, my cheeks wind-burned and nose chapped. Often I found snow tucked away in corners of my snowsuit that defied the laws of physics. But it was worth it, every crazy minute of it, and as I think of it now my heart swells.

The front door of the pizza parlor swung open and my father walked in. He stood in the front entryway, scanning the room. I made no motion to indicate I'd seen him. He found us and, with a hearty wave, joined us in the booth. He smelled faintly of cigarettes—odd, since he didn't smoke. I figured he'd met his client at a bar. He always smelled of smoke after he'd been to one.

He chatted amiably with us as we finished our snack, filching a sip of soda from me. That's when I noticed that he'd misbuttoned his Oxford shirt. He always buttoned them right up to the base of the neck, leaving only the top button free. Yet there were two buttonholes above that topmost button, making the collar of his shirt slightly askew. A simple mistake anyone could make, but I knew it hadn't been like that earlier. I saw it, yet I said nothing.

The following Monday my father came home from work and, as he did most every night, sat in front of the small Sony color television in the living room with a bottle of Schlitz beer in his hand watching the evening news. I sat beside him. The lead story concerned the American hostages in Iran. Last November fifty-two Americans had been taken hostage in the U.S. embassy in Tehran. So far little had been done. My father took this as evidence of President Carter's ineptitude.

My father lifted his beer bottle to his lips and drained its contents. "The peanut farmer screws it up again. Letting the Shah one-up us, just like the Ruskies. Way to go, Jimmy!" He turned to me. "Forget Russia. The next war will be with Iran, Jackie. Mark my words."

"Maybe we won't lose that one."

He fixed a steady gaze on me. "America has never lost a war."

"I don't know what you call Vietnam."

"We pulled out. It was a stalemate, a draw."

"There are no draws in war. You either achieve your stated objectives or you don't."

My father narrowed his eyes. "And what were the objectives of the Vietnam War?"

I pursed my lips. He had me there.

"Containing the spread of communism in Asia," he intoned, clearly pleased to be lecturing me. "If we hadn't stepped in, all of southeast Asia would be red right now."

"Saigon fell five minutes after we pulled out," my mother said. I hadn't seen her standing in the doorway. She stood with her arms crossed, one shoulder against the door frame. "Fifty-eight thousand dead American soldiers, and how many Vietnamese? How many women and children?"

"Now wait a minute," Dad said.

"America is an empire of blood," I said.

My father stood and jabbed a finger in the air at my mother. "Are you feeding him this crap?"

"I didn't tell him that."

"Well who did?"

"My teacher," I said.

"Jim Baird? He's a vet."

"He has a new teacher," Mom said. "Barbara Poindexter."

"You know her?" I asked.

She nodded. "We volunteer together at the DFL office. She's met Walter Mondale."

"Oh, great," my father muttered, shaking his head. "And now she's using the classroom to stump for Carter's re-election."

"It's healthy," Mom said. "Jackie will hear different views on things."

"Yeah, and he'll end up burning his draft card in Washington like your idiot brother," Dad said, throwing a hand up. "They should have tossed him in jail!"

"All right," my mother said. "That's enough. You men go and wash up. Dinner will be on the table in five minutes."

We ate in peace. Afterwards I helped my mother clean up in the kitchen. I heard the murmur of the television in the living room, where my father was ensconced again in his chair. I asked if my Uncle Vince had been a "conscious objector."

"Conscientious objector," she corrected. "Someone who refuses to fight in a war based on moral principles."

"Is he a pacifist?"

"Hardly. I've seen him pick plenty of fights."

"About what?"

"Girls. Liquor. The stupidest sorts of things."

"Do he ever go to jail?"

"No," she said with some surprise. "What makes you ask?"

I told her that Ms. Poindexter had mentioned a conscientious objector whom she knew, a man who'd refused to fight and who'd been jailed. I knew my Uncle Vince had protested the war, so I was wondering if he'd been jailed, too.

"Nothing that extreme." As she washed a bowl, she explained that Vince had protested the war there in Duluth, then in St. Paul, and finally out in D.C. It was true he'd burned his draft card, but nothing ever came of it. His number never came up. He never had to take that stand. But she thought he might have, if it had come to that.

This excited me, this hint of protest and defiance. I wanted to know more but at that point my father announced that *Laverne & Shirley* was on next, so we hurriedly finished up in the kitchen and took our places for our favorite show.

5

That spring, with my mother in school, our house had a different rhythm. Three days a week my mother was home when I got home, just as she'd always been, though she was not as quick to provide me with a snack or ask how my day had been. I was left to fend for myself in the food department, and I had to seek my mother out quietly if I needed to speak with her, for she was almost always buried deep in a book, or working on a paper. She seemed to write an awful lot of papers. I loved to spy on her during those sessions. She sat at the dining room table under an antique chandelier, her note cards and hand-written rough drafts spread around her like a set of surveyor's maps. She always wrote her drafts in pencil, frequently sharpening her preferred instrument: a yellow Dixon Ticonderoga No. 2. She sat elegantly at the table, back straight and erect, head lilting ever-so-slightly to one side, writing in her graceful, smooth script. My mother had gorgeous handwriting, very refined. (In contrast, my father had a crude, blocky style of printing—he never used cursive—that made everything he wrote look like a list of machine parts.)

When my mother had completed a handwritten draft of her paper it was time to move to the typewriter, a huge black Underwood that made a terrific clacking as she banged out her final draft. During this crucial phase I was not to interrupt her. This was the era when a mistake on the typewritten page entailed a complete cæsura in the process of composition: scrolling the typewriter cylinder up so that the offending line of type was above the keys and ribbon, fastidiously erasing the error (or, if that got too messy, simply bathing it in Wite-Out), and then carefully re-aligning the line in question and retyping. My mother was an absolute perfectionist with these papers, taking great pride not only in writing them but in presenting clean, error-free work. "Top shelf stuff," she liked to call it. Her professors must have agreed; she rarely scored anything below an "A."

The final stage of the writing process was always to read the paper aloud, going over everything one more time, checking for errors and, as she put it, "infelicitous verbiage." This she said with a smile; I never heard her accuse herself of this infraction. Even if my young ears could have recognized a maladroit phrase, it wouldn't have mattered. I was the most rapt of audiences. My mother promenaded slowly around the oval-shaped dining room table, pencil in hand, holding her paper up before her, occasionally pausing to emphasize a point. It was as if she were reading to a lecture hall. She had a warm, welcoming voice, and she read in a full-throated, sonorous oratory that filled the olive-colored dining room. I especially liked to watch her mouth move as she read. My mother had a beautiful mouth. Her lips, like mine, were full and robust, and red as an apple. She had a fine, angular jawline and a slender neck. She was a beautiful woman and I never tired of watching her.

I remember listening to her analysis of women in George Eliot, or morality in *The Mayor of Casterbridge*. Her history papers were even better: pithy analyses (to my untutored ears) of the overextension of the Roman Empire, or of ecclesiastical scholarship in the Dark Ages. If I didn't always understand what she was reading (and I rarely did) she would explain it to me later in the kitchen as she prepared supper. She was eternally patient with my questions. That, as much as anything, endeared those afternoons to me, and gives me now—forty-something, stewed in whiskey and nostalgia, hunched over this laptop—the full sense of what was lost.

Tuesday and Thursday afternoons were another matter entirely. On those days my mother had a late afternoon class and didn't arrive home until five o'clock. I became a latch-key kid, entrusted to come home directly from school at three, fix myself a snack, and see to my homework. I did no such thing. I found countless reasons to loiter on my walk home, stopping off at the Mount Royal drug store to purchase a package of mints and browse the magazines. When I did get home I helped myself to colossal portions of peanuts, soda crackers, licorice, and potato chips. If I was truly hungry I made a sandwich. I ate in front of the television, flipping between game shows, soap operas, and afternoon talk shows, my favorite being Mike Douglas. Then there was the four o'clock movie on KDLH, hosted by local weatherman Jack McKenna. I watched Ma and Pa Kettle, the Marx Brothers, Abbott and Costello, and Charlie Chan. But the best was always Sherlock Holmes, starring the incomparable Basil Rathbone in his cloak and deerstalker. Of course my mother had made me swear to "no television" when setting the rules, and so I would have to turn the television off at minutes to five, acting sweet and lovely when she got home, assuring her that my homework was complete and my chores taken care of, and could I please, please, please watch one hour of television before dinner? With a little luck I would have missed only a few minutes of the movie.

On other afternoons I rifled through my father's record collection. His hifi was in his basement office. I'd cue up Elton John's *Greatest Hits*, Jim Croce's *I Got a Name*, or *Bridge Over Troubled Water* by Simon and Garfunkel, and proceed to snoop through his desk drawers and filing cabinets. My father had a beautiful roll-top desk with all sorts of small drawers and cubby holes filled with strange-looking rocks, stray nuts and bolts, beer coasters, and lots of mail and bills. His file drawers were filled with manila folders and envelopes, bank statements and tax information. I found the file on his Pontiac, complete with the paperwork for the loan, and his honorable discharge from the Air Force.

It was on one such afternoon that I discovered, in the back of a file drawer, wedged between two manila folders, a thick, glossy magazine. Splayed across the top in blue capital letters was the word *PENTHOUSE*. A busty woman in a tank top graced the cover, her nipples jabbing like pencil points. I'd seen this magazine on the drug store shelves wrapped in black plastic. I knew it was dirty or illicit though I had never actually seen its pages.

I opened the magazine. Glossy pictures of naked women in startling poses leapt up at me. One lady, dressed like a firefighter, wrapped the hose around herself in curious ways. Another set of pictures showed two girls kissing and touching each other. There was something oddly captivating about these images. I stared at them for a long, long time. They excited me in a strange way. I felt unstable, a little berserk, actually. I wanted to put the magazine away, yet I couldn't stop turning the pages. I unfolded the glossy poster. I pored over the photos of women sprawled on beds, or washing themselves in the shower. I studied a couple making love, limbs entwined. When I'd finished I stuffed the magazine back into the nether regions of the file drawer. It occurred to me that I didn't remember how it had been placed there: front or back facing in or out, binding up or down. I worried that if I didn't place it back exactly like my father had left it my transgression would be discovered and I would be punished.

I spent the afternoon in a kind of funk. Something about those photos felt dirty and wrong, yet I couldn't stop thinking about them. After a half-hour of trying to forget them I ran back to my father's office and took out the magazine and looked at them all over again, scrutinizing the details with animal ferocity.

Back in my room, the proverbial black cloud hung over my head. I wished I'd never found the magazine. I couldn't quit thinking about those pictures, couldn't get them out of my mind. They frightened me, with their bold provocation and desperate, aching nakedness. I'd never seen anything quite like them. Did all adults do the things I'd seen in those pictures? Did everyone like that stuff?

When I was very young I had a fantasy that another, alien world existed around me. The adults in my life—my parents, my grandparents, my teachers—were actually monsters with terrible, hairy faces and sharp claws. When they were around me they donned masks that made them look human. They behaved in loving ways and pretended to care for me, but when they closed the bathroom door, or when the lights went out at night, or when they drove off in the car the first thing they did was tear off the masks, which were painful to wear, reverting to their true and terrible nature. I knew this, yet I could never acknowledge it or ask them to remove their masks for fear of them destroying me.

The feeling I had that afternoon, after looking through my father's dirty magazine, was similar. I had seen behind the mask, seen the true nature of the people around me, revealed in startling detail. Or had I? Even then, it occurred to me that those photos might be a kind of lie. My father was certainly capable of disingenuity. He wore a mask every day when he drove off to Weimann & Brothers in his sports coat and polished leather shoes. The charming salesman that the housewives met was not my real father; he was an imposter, a charlatan, a man posing as something other than who he was, or wanted to be.

All of this confused me. I knew I should never see those terrible photos again. I should try to put them out of my mind and forget all about them. Yet, the more I tried, the more the images assaulted me. I wanted to see them, I wanted the feeling I got while looking at them, that wild, tremulous buzz.

In my bedroom I lay on my bed with the shades pulled low. In the dim light I studied the pattern on my wallpaper: two vertical lines with a succession of fleur-de-lis, one on top of the other, from floor to ceiling. It looked like the bars of an iron gate obscured by fog.

The next day, a Saturday, I moped around in my room, still in a funk. My mother was out somewhere. My father was downstairs in the living room watching television. He called to me, telling me to come down and see a show on the Berlin Airlifts. I trudged downstairs slowly, one hand on the wall, and slinked into the armchair across from him. On the television screen giant aircraft flew low over the buildings of West Berlin, dropping much-needed supplies to the Berliners trapped there, surrounded by the Soviets and East Germans, their roadways and rail lines cut off. The footage was spectacular. The graceful, silver-winged airplanes dropped some five thousand tons of food a day into the embattled city. Grateful West Berliners rushed to unpack the crates as children waved to the NATO pilots. The dour East German soldiers stood at their checkpoints, staring at their Western brethren through tangled strands of barbed wire. Never had an air campaign like it been organized. The Soviets were utterly thwarted, eventually relenting, re-opening the roadways and rail lines to West Berlin, a small island of democracy and hope, its citizens stalwart and brave in the face of overwhelming opposition. It was enough to make one weep.

Ordinarily I would have rejoiced to watch the show. But as I sat there that afternoon all I could think about was that dirty magazine and those photos. The fact that it belonged to my father disturbed me. It seemed that I did not know the man, that there was something about him I could not understand or love. He seemed utterly strange to me. Yet, even in the midst of that funk, I understood the problem wasn't just my father—it was those photos. It was me! Why, if the images were so disturbing, could I not stop thinking about them? The fact that I kept going through them in my mind, remembering every last contour, every breast and thigh, every painted eyelash…. Oh, it drove me mad, and the hell of it was that I was the one thinking these thoughts. My father might have owned the photos, and that might make him some kind of a scoundrel, but what was I? I was a wreck. I was diseased.

I watched the television show for fifteen minutes, then complained of a headache and climbed back upstairs, closing my bedroom door behind me. I cued up a favorite 45 on my little turntable, set it to repeat, and crawled into bed and shut my eyes, willing myself to disappear into the song which could not fail to take me far away for three minutes and thirty-seven seconds.

Over the weeks Poindexter slowly made the classroom her own. Down came Baird's pictures of American flags flying over Congress, or the Navy's Blue Angels soaring in tight formation. Now we had Dr. Martin Luther King, Jr. and Bob Dylan on the walls. Each time she put a photo up we had a little lesson on who this person was. We watched a film of the "I Have a Dream" speech. We sat around a bulky record player listening to "The Times They Are A-Changing" and "The Ballad of Hollis Brown." Most of the kids found this boring, but for me every lesson was a precious unfolding.

My private sessions with Poindexter continued. Two afternoons a week, while the other students were watching television, or witnessing a demonstration of the warm and plangent oboe, I sat alone with my teacher, concentrating on math exercises. We always sat beside each other, behind her desk. She made me want to try, and I did improve.

One afternoon I managed to complete a worksheet in half the time it usually took, making just one mistake. I corrected it and handed it back. While Poindexter reviewed my work I studied her thick rope of necklaces strung with small, brown beads. Only they didn't exactly look like beads. They looked like dried boogers. This seemed strange. After she handed back my work I asked her about her necklace.

Poindexter held the ropes up. She told me that the necklace was from Africa. It was made of bread dough. She explained how they rolled out the dough, dried it, and then used it to make jewelry.

This amazed me. "Why do they do that? Aren't people starving in Africa?"

A gentle smile formed at the corners of her mouth. "Yes, in certain areas. But Africa is a very large continent. I don't think many people are starving where this necklace came from in Kenya. I was given this by a good friend. Here, smell it."

She lifted the thick braid and held it forward. I leaned over, and though it seemed like I was about to breathe in a big whiff of somebody's nasal discharge, I inhaled. The beads carried a delicate aroma, an earthy smell with a hint of musk, at once mysterious and completely familiar.

Poindexter lifted the necklace to her nose, closed her eyes, and inhaled slowly.

"When I smell these beads I see the village where I lived for two years," she said. "It's very far away, but it seems a little closer when I smell these beads."

She picked up a framed photo from her desk and handed it to me. Poindexter stood in the middle of a long line of black people. The men wore trousers and dress shirts with sweaters; the women had colorful skirts and blouses. They stood before a small house with a tin roof. Behind the house stood dark green mountains, crowned in silver mist.

"These are the teachers from the school where I worked," she said. "I lived outside of Nukuru, in the Rift Valley, near a beautiful lake. I taught English at a high school there."

Growing up in Duluth I'd seen few minorities of any kind, save for the reservation Indians. Finns, Poles, Scots and Swedes—that's what passed for racial diversity in northern Minnesota in the Seventies.

"Maybe one day you'll think about traveling," she said. "Have you done much of that?"

I told her I'd been to Minneapolis to visit relatives, and I'd been to Bemidji and Thunder Bay for hockey tournaments. Every summer my dad took me camping in the Boundary Waters, if that counted.

Poindexter asked if I'd ever thought about leaving North America on a trip, seeing some other, far-off corner of the world, like Africa or Asia.

"Thought about, sure."

"Where would you go, Jackie?"

The answer was easy. "Russia."

"Really. Why there?"

"I want to know why they hate us. I want to know why they want to blow us all to bits."

Poindexter frowned. "You think that's true?"

I gave her a look like she was nuts. They must hate us, I argued, since they had more tanks, guns, planes and missiles than anyone, and they were all pointed at us.

"Haven't you ever wondered if there are some people there who don't hate us?" she asked. "Some children like you who are simply curious and might want to be friends?"

Maybe, I said, but they weren't the ones aiming the missiles, and that's who I was worried about.

Poindexter agreed, but said there was more to it. I was focusing on fear, and fear was what kept the missiles on red alert. There were other ways of looking at it. For instance, had I heard of SALT II?

My puzzled face answered for me.

Poindexter explained how, just last year, President Carter had negotiated an arms limitation treaty with the Soviet Union reducing the stockpile of existing weapons and restricting the construction of new missiles.

"What does that tell you?"

I shrugged my shoulders. All I knew about President Carter I'd heard from my dad, who'd never recovered from the fact that Carter had canceled the B-1 bomber, one of many decisions that led to the closing of numerous Air Force bases, Duluth among them. "I wouldn't be selling pots and pans if it weren't for that peanut farmer," was a typical comment from my father. I wasn't about to repeat that to Poindexter.

"Here's what it tells me," she said. "They don't want to blow us up any more than we want to blow them up." She leaned closer to me and, in a soft voice, said, "There are reasonable people on both sides, Jackie. They just don't happen to be in charge of things. But you have to believe that somewhere in Russia there's a boy your age, just like you, wondering if everyone in America hates him. And we know that isn't true, don't we?"

We did. Poindexter's argument seemed irrefutable, even if it completely contradicted my father's views. I didn't know what to make of the schism. The world seemed much broader and more complicated than I'd ever imagined; a somber silence was the result. A few minutes later I was dismissed, and I carried this silence out to the playground, where the petty games of who-captured-who suddenly seemed barbaric and pointless.

* * *

My mother was under the crunch, working like mad to complete her mid-term papers and study for her tests. Because working at home on the weekends was impossible—Dad and I were too loud and interrupted her too much—she headed off to campus to work in peace and quiet at the library. One Saturday afternoon she returned later than expected. I came downstairs to grab a cola out of the fridge. (My mother was a big fan of the Elf brand; our fridge was usually stocked full of orange, black cherry, root beer, and lemon-lime.) Dad was laying into Mom, asking what had taken her so damn long. His voice seemed unnecessarily loud and confrontational, like he was trying to corner her. He sounded weird.

She told him she'd been right where she'd said she'd be, at the university library, researching her literature paper. She'd taken notes for three hours, gone out for a sandwich, and returned to start her first draft.

I asked what she was writing about.

"Henry James and the New Woman," she said, without looking at me. "Isabel Archer in *The Portrait of a Lady*."

I wanted to ask her to read me some of what she'd written, but clearly this wasn't the right time.

My father took down his bottle of bourbon from the cupboard and poured himself a splash. "You're spending too much time on all this stuff."

My mother gave him a long, hard look.

"What's the matter with you? I'm getting an 'A' in that class. In both of my classes. You should be proud."

He leaned against the kitchen counter, swirling his drink. "I don't see the point."

"Then you're not going to like what I have to tell you."

"And that would be?"

She wanted to start full-time in the fall. She'd spoken with a counselor. They'd gone over the entire process, from the due dates to how to apply for loans to—

"What about Jackie?" my father blurted.

"He's already coming home on his own two days a week."

"That needs to end."

"Dad, it's fine," I said. "I can handle it."

He jabbed a finger at me. "Stay out of this."

"Don't talk to him like that," Mom said.

"I'll talk to him any way I want. I'm his father."

"How much whiskey have you had?"

"That has nothing to do with it."

"Answer my question."

"Don't change the topic!"

My mother crossed her arms and gave him a fine, withering look worthy of Ava Gardner. "Why do you have a problem with me going to school?"

"I have a problem with my son coming home to an empty house while his mother is off chasing a college degree. A degree she doesn't need because she has a husband who works to pay the bills."

"Oh, we're back to that, are we? You feel threatened because your wife wants to get a college degree and you never got one."

Dad took a long, slow sip off his drink. "I didn't want a college degree."

"So why do you care if I want one?"

"You don't need one."

"I didn't say I needed one, I said I wanted one."

Now it was Dad's turn to glare. "If you think I'm going to pay for it, you've got another thing coming."

Mom shrugged her shoulders. "I'll get a loan."

"And pay it back how?"

"I'll get a job when I graduate."

"With a degree in English?" My father laughed. "Like some banker downtown needs you to explain *Hamlet*."

That set off a whole new round of arguing, which gradually escalated until they were shouting at each other. I was ordered upstairs. I assumed my customary position near the top of our L-shaped stairwell, just around the corner and out of sight, but in prime position to listen to my parents shout names and curses at each other. They were no longer trying to be civil, no longer discussing anything, really. They were just shouting, their voices shrill and full of anger. It's the kind of thing that makes a kid's gut twist up tight, the kind of thing that finally registers as deep fear, for even a child knows that nothing good can come of it.

This time, however, it didn't end with my father storming into the basement, or my mother flying to her bedroom. It ended with a terrific, glass-shattering slamming of the back door. Moments later my father started the car and raced backward out of the driveway, pulling onto Arrowhead Road. I listened as the roar of the Pontiac faded from our street.

A haunting silence descended on the house. After several minutes I made my way downstairs to the kitchen. My mother sat at the table. She had a vacant, wasted look on her face, like she'd just been punched in the gut.

"Where did he go?"

She shook her head. "To a bar, probably. I don't know."

On the counter stood the bottle of bourbon and my father's drink, half-finished. I poured his drink down the drain. I wanted to pour out the bottle, too, but I'd catch holy hell for that. The bourbon went back up in the cabinet.

Mom cleaned up the glass in the back hallway—a small pane had shattered—and taped a piece of cardboard over the hole to keep out the cold. Then we sat down at the kitchen table, across from each other, and waited.

I remember the day I lost my mother in Glass Block, a large department store downtown. I was just four years old. I found myself wandering through the men's clothing section, blindly turning corners and calling out. We were separated for just a few minutes, but in that time I felt terror and confusion, a panic wholly new to me. I've never forgotten the cold, deep tightening in my gut, the throbbing in my head, the way each detail of fabric—hanging trousers, pressed shirts, belts hanging like gutted snakes from a toothed rack—took on a savage sharpness.

The relief I felt on being reunited with my mother was so total, so complete, I would come to cherish the entire event despite my terror if only to savor that one brilliant, ecstatic hug, both of us in tears, clinging tightly to one another, vowing it would never, ever happen again.

My father came home well after midnight. I heard him stumble around downstairs, running the tap in the kitchen and humming a little tune. He made his way up the wooden staircase, clomping like an ox. After a few minutes in the bathroom he walked down the hallway and entered the master bedroom.

"Go sleep on the couch," I heard my mother say.

"I will not."

"Then I will." The bed springs creaked.

"Get back in that bed. I want to talk to you."

"Don't touch me."

"I'll touch you if I want to."

"No, you won't. And don't talk to me like that."

"What the hell is wrong with you?"

"You're so full of shit it makes me sick."

I heard a thumping and the sound of something heavy crashing to the floor. My mother shrieked.

"Mom!" I called out. "Are you all right?"

"Stop it, you bastard!" my mother snarled. "Let go of me! You're frightening Jackie!"

The fracas ceased. There was a long silent pause, heavy as an anvil.

"It's all right, son," my father said.

My mother stomped off down the hall. She stepped into my room and sat on the edge of the bed. She tucked me in, brushing her fingers across my brow. She let out one wet sniffle. She was crying, and she was trying to hide it from me.

"Mom, I'm scared."

"Don't be. Your father wouldn't hurt me. Not like that."

"What's going on? What are you guys arguing about?"

"We'll talk about it later. I'm going downstairs, okay? You get some sleep now. It's going to be all right, I promise."

Then she kissed my brow and left me. In the darkness of the house I heard all three of us, alone. Separate. Downstairs, my mother quietly wept and blew her nose. In his bedroom my father mumbled in a low voice, arguing with his ghosts before dropping off to sleep, snoring like a longshoreman. And me, staring wide-eyed into the pitch black darkness surrounding me, scared and uncertain, wondering what it all meant, what it would lead to. I had friends whose parents had divorced. I knew about that. I wondered if this is how it started, or ended, one of the two.

That night I dreamt of a woman in white, wearing a pearl choker. She was a little older than me but we knew each other, we had some sort of history. Our love was illicit, dangerous in some way, yet we'd remained true to one another despite our worries. We'd been apart for a long time and our reunion brought great joy to both of us. We picnicked in a pasture alongside a forest, near a fallen tree, a great red cedar. This wasn't Minnesota, I gradually realized. It was Russia. I was there, in that foreign and dangerous land, visiting my girlfriend.

We spoke, each word radiant and meaningful, pulling us closer. We nuzzled and kissed. She stroked the back of my neck, her touch electrifying. Her hand traveled across my chest, down my belly, past the waistline of my trousers, moving ever lower.

Uncontrollably, a warm wetness poured out onto my belly.

I awoke in the dark, startled, panting for breath. It took a few seconds for my senses to register and my confusion to clear, for the extraordinary power of that dream to dissipate. That girl, already fading in my mind—

What was her name? How did I know her? I wanted so badly to return to her.

I clicked on the lamp beside my bed. I stared blankly at the small, milky white puddle on my stomach. I didn't recognize myself. It didn't register that this had happened to me. I had become strange to myself, and I wept.

125

6

One weekday afternoon John Skoglund and I rode our bikes out Woodland Avenue to the Glen Avon playing fields to hit grounders to one another and work our gloves on a real infield. Tryouts for the Juniors were coming up, and while I knew John felt confident and ready, I was anything but. A low, tight feeling had settled deep in my gut, the worst of portents. At age twelve I'd learned at least this much: an athlete who lacks confidence, no matter how skilled, is doomed to fail.

We were just twenty minutes into our practice when Marta Haugen and Carrie Walczak showed up. I watched the girls lean their bicycles against the chain-link fence. Marta wore a red plaid knee-length skirt, navy stockings, and a white blouse. Her braided hair brushed her shoulders. She looked adorable.

John walked over to me when he saw the girls approaching and handed me the ball.

"Change of plan," he said.

"You set this up," I said, trying not to sound nervous.

"I told them we'd be here, is all. Come on, we'll have some fun."

Carrie was the shortest girl in sixth grade. She had shoulder-length black hair and a rough, husky voice that made her sound like a teenager. She had the sharpest, loudest laugh I'd ever heard, the kind that turned heads. Despite this, she was extremely popular. John made a big show about going with Carrie. Everyone admired him for it.

John announced that he knew a spot where his older brother and his high school friends partied. Keen to uncover the mysteries of teenagers, the four of us walked off behind the hockey rinks at the far end of the park. In late March the white boards looked battered and forlorn, the rinks' corners still covered in wasted patches of ice and snow. Scraggly tufts of bright spring grass peppered the ground, the most delicate kind of defiance.

We climbed a foot path into a stand of birch and elm on a hillside, their branches still bare. The ground was soft and slightly damp from the snow melt. John led us into a clearing in the small grove, in the center of which stood a fire pit surrounded by stones, filled with ashes and charred beer cans. Cigarette butts and stray bits of trash littered the area.

John pulled a pack of cigarettes out of his pocket. We watched him light one with a kitchen match, his head cocked coolly to one side. He took a short puff and held it, exhaling with a knowing grin.

He held the pack out. "Anybody want a smoke?"

"Where did you get those?" Carrie asked.

"I know some people."

I recognized the blue-and-red target on the pack. They were Vantages, which his mother bought by the carton. It would be easy enough to filch a pack from Jeanette Skoglund. But I didn't say anything. I watched as both Carrie and Marta took cigarettes, and though I had never in my life seriously thought about smoking, I took one, too. John lit a match and held it for the girls, who inhaled with rapid, short puffs.

He tossed me the book of matches. "Burn it up, Rose."

We stood in a circle, watching each other as we took quick, light drags, immediately exhaling. John shook his head.

"You have to hold the smoke in."

Taking a short puff, he managed to suck it down and hold it for several seconds before exhaling with a slight cough. It was impressive, sure, and maddening as hell, because he'd obviously been practicing, thinking of just such a moment. It was that calculation, that planning and scheming, that made him foreign to me, more like his older brother and less my peer, deepening my discomfort.

The rest of us tried to imitate John's example. Immediately, Carrie, Marta and I were hacking our lungs out, staggering around the clearing while John laughed. Red faced, my lips wet with spit, I resumed taking my short, antiseptic puffs, feigning enjoyment. But really I craved an orange Elf soda to wash the horrible taste from my mouth.

John's next bombshell was that he knew how to sneak into the club house down by the rinks, a smelly old box of a building with rubber mats covering the floors for the ice skaters, really just a dressed-up warming shed. There was a pathetic little snack bar that sold soda, popcorn, and candy. On sub-zero nights we all but ran for the club house between periods, our fingers and toes stinging with cold, faces red with exertion. The whistle that summoned players back to the rink was a black signal of pain.

John led us behind the building, beneath a window that could be jimmied open. Lacing his fingers together, he squatted down to help boost the girls up through the window with relative ease. Then he jumped up and, gripping the sill, hauled himself up through the window. His impish face appeared a moment later.

"Come on, Jackie, get in here or I'll have two girls to myself!"

His face disappeared and a wave of giggles poured out the open window. I was determined to scamper up the side of that building if it killed me. I was a lean and limber boy, not especially strong, but I was light. I threw myself at the wall, managed to grasp onto the sill, then began flapping my feet, desperate for a hold. A conduit ran along the corner of the house. The toe of my shoe found purchase along the narrow seam of a joint. Hanging awkwardly, I took a deep breath and managed to lift myself up and through the window. I tumbled into a store room, crashing into a cardboard box of wax paper cups which spilled out over the floor. I looked up, expecting to see John looming over me, but found only Marta Haugen.

I asked where John and Carrie had gone.

"Who cares?" she said. "Let's you and me explore."

We walked out into the dim hallway. The rubber mats on the floor were clean. The thought that someone had mopped the place after the final game of the season seemed oddly surprising. Who should care for this place? I'd already written it off, having played my last game at Glen Avon. Next season I'd be in the Bantams, playing on the high school rink. I thought I'd seen the last of this club house, yet here I was creeping around inside it with a girl.

Marta and I walked slowly down the hallway, past the locked-up snack counter, past the restrooms. My heart thumped with adrenaline. Every step seemed illicit. Our very presence here constituted a crime, a thought that both frightened and tantalized me.

The two team rooms dominated the building. Glen Avon's was the one closest to the bathrooms and snack bar. It was here that we laced up our skates and donned whatever gear we hadn't put on before arriving. It was usually a crowded, hot, noisy place that smelled of sweat, its wet floors strewn with gear bags and winter boots. Now the room looked barren and empty, its rows of battered wooden benches in wobbly, uneven lines.

Marta took my hand. We peered around the corner into the next room. John and Carrie were sitting on a bench. Carrie leaned against the wall, her feet crossed demurely at the ankles. John leaned over her, his face close, his right hand slowly kneading her hip. For a long moment I watched only it, wondering where it would go next.

Marta tugged on my hand, hauling me into the next room. She gave me a quick peck on the lips. Our eyes met. I held her stare. Meeting this small challenge emboldened me. I felt one degree stronger, braver. Still I trembled, a quiver that started in my shoulders and traveled down my arms to my fingertips. I knew I didn't have to go through with anything. A few words, or simply walking away, it could be that easy. But it wasn't that easy. I sensed I was on the edge of something, and part of me wanted to go there.

We sat on one of the stout green benches in the middle of the room. Marta touched my shoulder, her fingers light and soft. I wanted so badly to touch her, if that was the right thing to do. I wanted to know the right thing to do. Marta leaned in, her face hovering before mine, her ripe rose lips and cool blue eyes so very close. She stared into me with a sharpness I couldn't match.

She kissed me again. I sat dumbfounded, frozen like a stupid animal.

"Kiss me back," she whispered.

And so I did.

She kissed my cheek, and then my neck, just under the ear. I kissed her back in those same places. And though I didn't know what I was doing, it all seemed hot and close and lush. This went on for some time, the minutes a heady blur, until she took my hand in hers.

"We're going to play doctor," she announced. "I want you to examine me."

Marta reclined on a neighboring bench. She looked beautiful there, her blonde tresses laid out beside her head, her legs out straight, two knobby knees side-by-side.

"Go ahead, doctor."

I touched a trembling fingertip to the underside of her chin, pressing gently at the soft flesh there. Marta closed her eyes. Inhaling sharply, she lifted her chin, inviting me to continue. I moved my finger slowly, skating across the collar of her shirt, to the tips of her shoulders and down her arms, speckled with faint brown freckles. I brought it back to the bony V of her collarbone. I stopped there, unsure how to proceed.

Marta guided my hand to the soft mound of her breast. Her chest rose as she breathed. Her breast was soft. Under one finger I felt the strap of her bra. She seemed so calm! I held my hand there, immobile, unsure what else I might do, how much further I might go.

Marta flipped the hem of her skirt up, revealing crème yellow panties with white trim. A little orange flower, a Gerber daisy, was embroidered on one hip. I stared at this flower, thunderstruck. She wanted me to touch her, to touch her underwear.

I swallowed, willing myself to be brave. Hands shaking, I pinched the waist band of her panties between finger and thumb and lifted it. Thin red lines, the impression of fabric on skin, were the first things I saw. I pulled the panties lower, exposing a wisp of pubic hair. I stared hard at it, my throat tight and heart racing. Did she really want me to touch her there? I couldn't do it, I just couldn't. I let go, the elastic of her panties snapping back into place.

Marta slowly adjusted her skirt, then sat up beside me on the bench. I couldn't look at her, my eyes blind, my mind as blank as a Russian steppe.

"Now it's my turn," she said, softly. "Lay on your back and the nurse will examine you."

I lay back on the bench, staring up at the stippled daubs of ceiling plaster, searching for a pattern, a design, a recognizable image: it seemed an inscrutable mess. If I'd been nervous a moment ago, I was beyond that now. Blood thrummed in my skull. I felt somehow outside of myself, present but not understanding.

Marta's fingers traced their way up my forearm to my shoulders and neck, then down my Adam's apple and to my collarbone. Her fingers moved slowly along my ribs, the quivering marsh of my abdomen. They stopped at the waistband of my jeans, her fingertips digging just beneath. Inside my pants my erection throbbed. My breath came short and fast, an animal panting.

She unsnapped the button at the top of my jeans, then tugged at the difficult zipper. She peeled back the denim like a butcher unwrapping a fresh cut of meat. Tracing a finger along the elastic band of my white underwear, she told me that the nurse needed to look in there.

With a quick tug, she pulled the front of my underwear down. My erection sprang free, hovering in mid-air. I looked not at it but at the face of Marta Haugen, who studied it with a clinician's cool indifference. She placed her fingertips very lightly on my thigh, a butterfly's caress. She leaned closer. "It's so funny," she said.

Then her hand moved.

For one moment, one stunningly bleak and clear second, something stood before me. Perceived so clearly, and from so very near, it had no qualities at all. The recognition of it and the consciousness of the vision's clarity left no room on the mind's horizon. Then a shadow moved deep inside, covering another, darker shadow, a black churning swirl, raw and terrifying.

Brushing her hand away, I abruptly pulled up my underwear and stood, lightheaded, erection throbbing, fumbling with the zipper of my jeans. I bolted out of the room and down the hall. Marta called my name but I did not turn or answer her. I rushed into the store room and clambered up and into the window. I leapt to the spongy grass below, one knee landing in a boggy puddle, the cold dampness soiling my jeans.

At my bicycle I lingered, entertaining second thoughts. Was I a gentleman or a fool, a nut case or a coward? I stared into a copse of alder and birch along the nearby creek. A sheet of newspaper was wrapped around the trunk of one tree, flush with the ground, a victim of spring flooding, a thing shaped by forces larger than itself, bleached of its original purpose and relevancy, destined only for slow decay.

I hopped onto my blue three-speed Schwinn and in seconds was racing down the dirt road, around the back of the hockey rinks and up onto Woodland Avenue. I pedaled madly, pumping until my thighs burned, jumping off curbs and darting across intersections, until finally I was at the top of Grass Hill. I plunged down the steep, broken sidewalk that ran along one side of the hill, relishing the gathering speed, trees whipping by in a blur.

I will never understand why I didn't reach for the hand brake sooner. When I did it was too late: I flew off the curb at the bottom of the hill, rocketing into the street. I turned sharply to avoid the opposite curb. The back wheel skidded out from under me and I went flying, crashing and tumbling head-over-heels until I came to rest in George Sundby's flower bed. There I lay for a second or a minute or an hour, I do not know. Faces swirled around me like angels in a dream, their voices inscrutable. A sharp stabbing sensation arose in my side, a red burning intensity. I thought I should sit up, but I could not move.

I broke my right arm in the crash and sustained a mild concussion. My body ached all over. After two days' bed rest I returned to school, where I immediately became the object of attention. This pleased me. I had prepared a version of my story, a gripping account of speeding down the long straightaway on Grass Hill faster than anyone had ever dared, staying on my bike as I bolted out into the road, crashing in a wild tumult on Old Sundby's lawn. There was no motive, in my account, other than the sheer love of speed and an inflexible courage. I repeated the story several times until all my classmates and friends had heard it. My strategy was successful. I was told I was wildly foolish, brave, and out of my mind: precisely the image I wanted for myself.

Marta Haugen listened along with the rest, quietly watching me with those icy blue eyes. She signed her name in red ink on my cast, then drew a heart around it. Without a word she smiled and turned away, content to let me bask in my hour of attention. I wasn't sure what to make of her silence; frankly, it mystified me. But I prayed for it to continue. With a word she could destroy me.

John Skoglund pestered me with questions. Why had I run away from the warming shed? How far had I gotten with Marta? And what was I thinking, racing down Grass Hill like that?

I waited until lunch recess to give him the details. As I spoke I realized my tale was not exactly untrue. I'd gotten to second base with Marta, I told him, and had charged right ahead to third. She could say the same.

"No fucking way."

"Ask Carrie," I said. "I'm sure she knows."

I was quiet, willing him to challenge me. He did not. But he still wanted to know why I'd bolted out of there.

It was a good question. My mind raced to find a convincing answer, one that would not undermine the now sterling story I had fashioned from the ruins of that afternoon.

Everything happened quickly, I said, our hands were all over each other. It was mad, it was crazy and I really really wanted to stay, but if I wasn't home before my mother returned from college I was toast, grounded for ages. I stayed in that shed soaking in every last moment, and let me tell you they were luscious. At the absolute last possible moment I burst out of there, pedaling home like a fury. And I nearly made it, but I pushed a little too hard. Grass Hill is an unforgiving master, we both knew.

John nodded, apparently satisfied.

I exhaled a long, contented sigh. It was the greatest story I had ever told, and now that I'd uttered it and people believed it, every word began to feel true. And wasn't it? I hadn't lied; I simply hadn't told the entire truth. In so doing I'd transformed defeat into victory. This was a profound realization for me, the most delicate of lessons.

During P.E. the next morning the kids bopped volleyballs in the cavernous gymnasium, their sneakers squeaking on the glossy wood floor. Sunlight poured through high cathedral windows, casting distended shadows on the wall. With my cast and sling I naturally had an exemption. I sat on the bleachers, watching. John stepped out of the line and stood beside me.

"Tell me more," he said.

"I already told you."

He demanded intimate details. I told him I'd touched Marta's breast and pulled down her underwear.

John's eyes widened. "You saw it."

I lifted my chin and gave him one regal nod. The look of awe on his face emboldened me.

"Then it was her turn," I said. "You won't believe it." Leaning forward, I motioned with a wag of my head for him to come closer. "She touched it."

John rubbed a hand across his brow. "Bullshit!"

"Ask Carrie. Ask Marta, if you've got the balls, you retard."

He slapped a palm against his volleyball. He'd had his hands on Carrie's titties a dozen times, sure, but he hadn't seen *anything* below the waist, let alone her seeing his. And then, holy shit, she'd touched it! How in fuck's sake had I *done* that?

The teacher blew the whistle and shouted for John to get back in rotation. He dutifully complied. I remained on my perch in the bleachers, feeling like a king. To have bested John in anything—but especially in this new thing—oh, I felt in that moment stronger than I'd ever felt.

Of course I worried John would question Marta. But what could she say? She could not refute me. Our versions could only differ in that bold touch—in truth, a fingertip pressed gently against the stem of my hard-on. I'd recoiled as if bitten by an asp, blind with shame.

But I had a feeling Marta would not betray me, that she would prove loyal.

I basked in my glory, the center of attention. Kids wanted to sign my cast, asked what it felt like wearing it, offered to carry my school books or my lunch tray, or simply begged for yet another retelling of the momentous crash. I loved every minute of it. After a couple of days the hubbub began to die down. Then Tommy Moore barfed in the waste can just before recess and the class's attention moved elsewhere.

Initially the cast was a burden. I'd broken my right arm, which meant I had to do everything with my left. My homework looked like it'd been written by a kindergartener, in shaky, uneven letters. When the monitors collected work I handed it in face-down, hiding my shame. No such luck when they handed it back. Echo Lindstrom stood before me, a puzzled look on her face, before bursting out with a guffaw. Thankfully, Poindexter took pity on me, personally returning my work after that, sparing me further humiliation.

Away from school, the cast brought other concerns. It itched like hell. It felt like something had crawled in there and was squirming around. I wanted to take a coat hanger and jam it down there, but the doctor had warned me about that. The best I could do was set the hair dryer on low and blow air down the cast. This brought little relief.

There were other things: learning how to eat left-handed, how to shower without getting my cast wet (not easy), and, most frustratingly, how to sleep in bed without laying on my cast. All of this took time, patience, and repeated experiments to master.

But I did master it.

It would be an exaggeration to say I grew to like wearing the cast, but not as much as you'd think. There was the near-constant stream of attention. Women, especially, often asked me, How did I break my arm? Did it hurt? When would the cast come off? Each moment presented itself as an opportunity: for braggadocio, if I wanted to retell my version of the story; for sympathy, if I wanted to complain; or for stoicism, if I wanted to project an air of being above it all. Wearing the cast became a procession of opportunities. I understood such moments were fleeting. I looked at the calendar, counting the weeks and days until the cast would come off and I would return to my previous life, an ordinary boy warranting no special attention. What then? I would have to find new tricks to capture people's attention.

In class, in the lunch room, on the playground at recess, Marta kept her distance. At first this didn't bother me. It was a relief not to face her questions, if she had any. But after a few days it became obvious she was avoiding me, just as I was avoiding her, and though I didn't exactly want to talk about what had happened on that day in the warming shed, I couldn't stop thinking about it. In my room at night I replayed the scene in my mind. It seemed both terrifying and ecstatic, monstrous and delicious. I feared it, whatever it was, yet I wanted more. Like a poor penitent on a medieval torture device, I felt pulled in every direction, and no matter which way I turned I saw Marta Haugen.

7

Ms. Poindexter asked me to stay after class one day. Immediately, a round of "ooos" arose among the students. I had no idea what Poindexter wanted, but her request gave me an air of mystery. I might just have a secret. No one wanted to find it out more than me.

In fact, she only wanted to return my math homework with a big gold star on it and a hug of congratulations. There wasn't a single error in the batch.

"Way to go, Jackie. You're getting there. You just keep at it."

Once again, breaking my arm seemed like a good thing. I did a little less running around and spent a little more time at the desk. Having Mom in school helped, too. We had study sessions, working across from each other at the dining room table.

"My mom's applying to college," I told Poindexter.

"You should be proud of her."

"My dad doesn't see the point. He says it's a waste of money."

Poindexter slowly shook her head. Earning a college degree might be a challenge, she said, and it was certainly expensive, but it was never a waste of money. Then she asked if I had plans to attend college.

I'd never thought about it. No one on either side of my family had a college degree.

"What do you want to do?" Poindexter asked.

I'd thought about working for NASA and becoming an astronaut. Or maybe a fighter pilot.

"Then you'd better keep up with the math. Both jobs require a lot of it."

"Just my luck."

She told me not to worry. I had the makings of a scholar. Though I was having trouble in math, she could tell I was an excellent reader and writer, and I had a knack for history.

"You should go to college," she concluded. "It's the best thing in so many ways."

"Where did you go to college?"

"I went to Carleton, in Northfield, and then the University of Minnesota, where I got my teaching certification."

"Where are you from?"

She smiled. "Duluth. Washburn is my *alma mater.*"

"Your what?"

"I was a student here at Washburn. Many years ago." She leaned toward me and said in a low voice, "You know the principal, Mr. Tarnowski? He was my fifth grade teacher."

I thought my eyes would pop out of my head. Poindexter burst out laughing.

"Where did you think I was from?"

"I don't know, but not here. You've lived a lot of places."

Poindexter began arranging papers on her desk. "Maybe you'll travel the world, too."

"I wish you could be my teacher next year."

Poindexter smiled. "I would like that, Jackie. I would like that very much."

"Can you ask Mr. Tarnowski?"

Smiling, she told me she didn't plan to be around next year. Her stay in Duluth was temporary, something to do between her visit in Africa and whatever was next. But she would miss me, I could be sure of that.

I didn't tell her that this news broke my heart. I left the classroom and found the playground deserted and the school busses gone. I walked home alone, slowly, wishing Mr. Baird could have gotten lung cancer earlier so we would've had Poindexter all year. The meanness of the thought startled me, and so I wished for it again, harder.

A quiet Saturday passed. My mother was at the library, working on another essay. My father clambered up and down his aluminum ladder, removing the winter storm windows and installing summer screens. I spent a good portion of the morning watching cartoons, then decided to go for a walk around the neighborhood. I had no plan or destination. I was thinking about Marta, wondering what I should do. We hadn't talked in a week. I had no idea if she was angry, spiteful, hurt, or what. Privately, I knew my flight from the warming shed had been cowardly and naïve; if I had it to do over again I would have willed myself to stay there. How much further might we have gone? I mulled this question at length, steeping it to the point of bitterness.

Knowing more trumps knowing less, I lectured myself: the fact of having *done* something, as opposed to merely wondering what might have happened, seemed to my twelve-year-old mind the adult way of viewing it. This was an important point for me, as I felt trapped by childhood.

No, that's not right. It's more like I was desperate not to consider myself a child, desperate to move through the awkward age of not-knowing, to pass into the territory of knowledge, which I equated with certainty. This distant realm seemed at once both tantalizing and inscrutable. I believed Marta had been there. She was a messenger bearing news. I wanted all of it.

I knew I must see her again. My motives seemed unclear. If I wanted anything from her, it was only a vague, confused bundle of desires. Part of it was sexual, though I wouldn't have been able to explain it that way at the time. Yet, she'd made a distinct impression; she was the only girl I'd ever touched or kissed, certainly the only girl who'd touched me, and frankly the only girl I knew who had even an iota of sexuality about her. I'd never thought of girls this way before, at least not consciously; Marta had no competition. With her a line had been crossed and, having crossed it, I wasn't so afraid to do so again. In fact I was eager for it.

But that wasn't all I wanted. I wanted to be able to go back to John Skoglund with another triumph. I wanted to boast, to crow, to lord it over him. Marta was the only way I knew how to do that.

On the following Thursday, a day when my mother would be on campus and I could loiter after school, I screwed up my courage and sent Marta a note asking her if I could take her for a treat after school. She returned it promptly with a big YES written inside a heart.

Thrilled, I ran to tell John. He looked at me, shrugged his shoulders, and said so fucking what.

"I'll let you know what happens," I said, trying to sound like I had big plans.

"Nothing's going to happen, douche bag," he said, turning away.

His reaction disappointed me, deflating whatever sense of grandiosity I'd built up in my head. As the hours ticked by my anxiety deepened. I began to doubt my feeble plan. I'd walk her to Smitty's Standard Oil, a small, oil-streaked relic of a filling station. Smitty had been there since the Fifties, and so had his décor and signage. But his vending machine had the cheapest soda in town, thirty-five cents for a Coke. Two Snickers would be another seventy cents. I'd filched exactly $1.53 from my piggy bank, all the cash I had.

By the end of the school day I'd worked myself into a frenzy. What if she laughed in my face? What in hell was I doing? Yet I knew I must follow through, for I had made one promise to myself: never to run away from Marta ever again.

We met at the flag pole. It was a chilly day, overcast and threatening rain.

Underdressed, Marta wore wool pants that hung an awkward inch above her red Mary Janes, a simple T-shirt, and a blue cardigan. She clutched her backpack against her chest. I wore my Glen Avon hockey jacket, big and bulky enough to cover my cast and sling, with my left arm in the coat sleeve. She looked at me with a smile and waited.

"Come with me," I said, grabbing her hand. We walked down Woodland Avenue, gossiping about the boys and girls in our grade. Marta was funny, talented at impersonations, and she had a wicked wit. Our chat put me at ease. (I have always loved to talk.) By the time we made it to the corner of Woodland and St. Marie Street it wasn't hard to proffer my meager proposal to this girl I both feared and adored.

If she replied, I missed it. Just as I spoke the words I noticed a plum-colored '72 GTO with a white vinyl roof pulling out of the parking lot of Erikson's Swedish Restaurant—the exact same car as my father's. I stared hard at it, realizing it *was* my father's car. What was he doing at Erikson's at three o'clock in the afternoon? He indicated a left turn, the direction of Arrowhead Road and our house.

A bolt of fear charged through my body. He could be home in two minutes. There'd be hell to pay if I wasn't there. But I doubted he was going home. Beside him in the car was a woman wearing cat-eye sunglasses and a head scarf tied at the chin. I stood frozen in place, both petrified and confused.

My father found his gap in traffic, pulled out onto Woodland Avenue, and was gone.

"Jackie?"

"I just saw my Dad."

"Where?"

I pointed to the Pontiac. "It's weird. He works until six. And he had someone with him."

"He's probably on his lunch break. My mom works downtown and when she gets a break she walks around the block. It's because she's a phone operator. She sits in a chair all day, answering one stupid call after another. It's the most boring job ever. What's your dad do?"

"He sells kitchen ware."

"That's a girl's job."

"Men can do it," I said, sharply. "He's good at it."

"Sure he is. Runs in the family." Her smile was sweet, her cherry mouth glossy with lipstick.

"Let me get you that soda," I said.

She frowned. "I said no."

"What?"

Rolling her eyes, she grabbed my hand and told me to follow her.

She marched me across the parking lot to the Mount Royal drugstore. Marta said we could get more than candy. She grabbed a *Cosmopolitan* off the magazine rack. "Get whatever you want!"

I wanted the new *Mad* magazine, but that seemed childish. I grabbed a *Motor Trend*. On the cover was a boxy looking sedan, something called a K-Car. "Will This 1981 Front-Drive Save Chrysler?"

In the candy aisle Marta grabbed all sorts of stuff—candy bars, Pop Rocks, Hot Tamales. "Go on, Jackie!"

I felt a little strange. Upstaged, for sure. Why was Marta buying me candy and magazines? How could she afford it?

We proceeded to the register. Marta dumped her pile on the counter. I added my *Motor Trend* and a solitary carton of Milk Duds. Marta took a green check out of her coat pocket and handed it to the clerk, who looked at it for several long seconds.

"What's this?"

"A check from my mother."

"You want to use this to pay for candy?" The clerk read the name on the check. "This check is written to Bridgette Sanders."

"That's me," Marta said.

I gave her a quick double-take, but Marta stood patiently, hands calmly folded atop one another, staring up at the lady.

"You said this check is from your mother."

Marta nodded. "It is."

"What's her name?"

"Donette Sanders."

"That's not the name on this check."

A dark, tight feeling formed in my gut. I wanted to get out of there, just turn around and walk away. Whatever Marta was up to, it didn't feel right.

"The name on the account is Eileen Hendricks."

"That's my aunt."

"Then the check is not from your mother."

"My mother asked my aunt to write me a check."

"For seven dollars and twenty-two cents." The clerk studied the check again. "This is two months old."

"It's for shoveling snow, taking out the garbage, stuff like that," Marta said, cool as stone. "I didn't want to spend it until now."

The clerk looked down at the small pile before us, then at Marta, and then at the check.

"I have to consult my manager. Just wait right there."

Marta stood calmly at the counter, hands folded and back straight. I was anything but calm. My heart raced, my palms were sweaty. Marta was lying, obviously. But I was confused. She was so calm, so sincere in her answers, maybe I was just missing something.

I studied the cover of her *Cosmopolitan*: "The Rise and Fall of the New Man." Perfect.

A manager came out with the clerk and the whole conversation was repeated. This man seemed stern and doubtful. I thought for sure he'd rip up the check, or phone the police. Marta kept smiling, bouncing on the balls of her feet, answering questions like it was no big deal.

Eventually the manager had her sign the check as Bridgette Sanders. The clerk rang up the order and even handed Marta two dollars in change.

In the parking lot outside, I asked Marta where she'd gotten that check.

"I swiped it from an old bitch."

"Won't she find out?"

"I don't care. They'll be looking for Bridgette Sanders, whoever that is. Come on, let's go eat this candy!"

We sat under the arch of the Congdon Creek bridge, on a little cement ledge. It had started to drizzle. The rocks and boulders, ordinarily a dark gray, were black on top, rivulets of water streaking down their sides. Marta had a pack of cards with a picture of the Las Vegas strip on the back, a night shot with the glitzy neon signs and a long queue of red tail lights filling the main drag. She shuffled the deck and we each drew a single card. Low card would have to choose, truth or dare.

I lost first and chose truth. Marta asked, "What's the worst thing you've ever done?"

"Looking at my dad's dirty pictures" leapt to mind, but I wasn't going to say that! "I don't know. Breaking my arm, maybe."

"That was nothing! You've done worse than that." She leaned over and socked me in my good arm, a surprisingly hard hit.

"All right. Give me a second."

From lifting a comic book at the drug store once, to lying to my mother about a sweater I'd deliberately "lost" (an ill-fitting, brown-and-blue monstrosity, hand-knit by my aunt in Pennsylvania), I had plenty to choose from. But one thing rose above the others.

I asked Marta if she remembered Chris Cook. She didn't, which surprised me. I thought everybody at Washburn knew the kid who came to school in the yellow jumpsuit, the black cape, and the red canvas high-tops. Last year my friend Jerry Gustafson and I were on a hockey team with Cook. Jerry was something of a problem kid, always mouthing off and getting into trouble. He actually punched a referee one time and our coach benched him. He missed the last game of the season, a playoff game, which we lost. Jerry somehow decided it was Cook's fault, though it wasn't, and one day he picked a fight on the school playground. Cook wouldn't harm a doodle bug, let alone defend himself. I decided I just couldn't watch it happen.

"I jumped my best friend," I told her. "I took a swing at Jerry before he could lay into Cook."

"What happened?"

I lost the fight, badly. Jerry beat the royal shit out of me, right there in front of everybody. I got a two-day suspension for starting the fight, but for Jerry it was worse. He had quite a history with the principal, and our fight was the last straw. Jerry was expelled from Washburn and transferred to the Palmer School, where the problem kids went, the ones who'd fallen off the rails: chronic fighters, kleptomaniacs, drug dealers, child mothers.

"Sounds like he had it coming," Marta said, sending a pebble into the creek with a flick of her finger.

Maybe, I said, but I still felt bad about it. Not so much because of what Jerry had wanted to do to Cook, but because, ever since being expelled, he'd disappeared. Nobody ever saw him. It was like he'd caught some disease. He didn't hang around with any of the old Washburn crew, though he still lived in the neighborhood. He hung out with his older brother Dean, an even bigger trouble maker, ignoring me and everyone else, just as we ignored him.

"That's the first time I've lost a friend like that," I said. "And it was me who threw that first punch. I've always wondered, What if I hadn't done it? What if I'd just let him whip Cook's ass? Maybe Jerry would still be at Washburn. Maybe he'd still be my friend."

I sat back. It was the first time I'd said any of that out loud. I'd seen Jerry once at Grass Hill last winter, after the first big snow. Nothing could keep him from barreling down that hill. He was there with his brother's crew. Jerry and I nodded to each other but didn't speak. He seemed like a completely different person, hanging with the older, bigger kids who smoked and cussed and pushed each other around. I knew then we'd never again be friends, not like we were.

Marta shuffled the deck and we drew new cards. She lost and chose a dare, which meant I had to come up with something for her to do. I must have given her a dumb-ox look, because she smiled and said, "Why don't you ask me to kiss you?"

And so she did, a quick peck on the lips. Desire and fear stirred in my gut, making me want simultaneously to grab her and kiss her back, and to turn and flee. But I wasn't going to flee. Never again.

143

I was relieved when, after losing the next hand, Marta chose truth. I immediately asked her a question that had long been on my mind: Why had she failed sixth grade last year?

She frowned and looked away. I thought she might refuse to answer the question. But then she spoke in a quiet, soft voice.

"It started when my Aunt Berta died."

It was Aunt Berta who'd raised Marta. Marta's mother had never married. She only ever dated jerks. Marta hardly knew her dad, a truck driver who lived somewhere in Wisconsin. For years Marta's mother had worked second shift as a waitress, before getting the telephone job. Her mom was always busy, always had something important to do. Anything other than Marta.

"Berta was the only person who ever really loved me."

"Your mom loves you."

"Not like Berta did."

I asked how she died.

Cancer. They didn't find it until it was too late. It all happened so quickly. After Berta died, Marta and her mother had to move out of the apartment. They moved into Eileen Hendricks's basement, some lady her mom knew from church.

"Hendricks," I said. "That's the name on the check."

"Yeah, I stole it from her. That woman is a nasty, wrinkled-up old bitch," Marta said. "Bossy and mean. I wouldn't do anything she told me to do. She treated me like a maid. I had all these chores, and I had to do them every day. We were living there basically for free, so it was part of the deal. But she was evil. She swatted me with a wooden spoon once because I walked too slow. Another time she wanted to know if I'd washed my hands before touching her high-and-mighty china. I said I had, but I hadn't. She dragged me to the sink and put my hand under scalding water, practically burned all my skin off. I kicked her that time.

"She was so mean, I quit doing her damn chores. We'd get in these big fights. When my mom was around, which wasn't much, Eileen played nice, acting like it was no trouble having us, but she let my mom know I wasn't holding up my end of the bargain. Then Mom would lay into me, telling me I had to be a good helper. She wouldn't listen when I told her what Eileen was doing, the names she called me, the pinches and slaps. She didn't believe me. So I ran away."

"You ran away from home?" This fact stunned me.

"That wasn't my home. That was just some lady's basement."

"Where'd you go?"

"Friend of mine's." That girl was off at the middle school now, along with all Marta's other friends. That was the worst part about being held back, she said. Watching all your friends leave for another school while you're stuck in elementary, trying to make new friends.

"Anyway, last year I quit doing school work. Didn't even go to school half the time. There were these other kids who would skip with me. We got into some trouble and then I couldn't stay with my one friend anymore so I went to another place, but I could only stay there for a few days and then I was just basically staying wherever I could. One of these moms tried to 'help me' and called the county or whoever. Suddenly they're threatening to put me in a foster home.

"My mom just cried and cried. She took me back and found us a place, an apartment above Asplund Hardware. That's where we live now."

I knew the place. A little mom-and-pop hardware store two blocks from our school, at the corner of Woodland and Oxford.

"But I'd missed too much school and my grades were horrible. They held me back after all that, but at least I got to stay with my mom."

"So when did you steal that check?" I asked.

"A few weeks ago. My mom said we needed to stop by Eileen's. I told her I didn't want to go but she insisted. So we go over there and, sure enough, Eileen acts so damn happy to see me. She and my mother sit down with a cup of coffee in the kitchen and I say I have to go to the bathroom, but instead I do a little snooping. That's when I found the check."

"Damn."

We listened to the white roar of the water.

A peculiar moment, as I think on it now. I was twelve then. I believed that the life you were born into would be your life for the rest of your life. You'd have your mom and dad and your green house on East Arrowhead Road and the neighbors you knew and the town you claimed as your own. All of that would soon change, and I had many hard lessons to learn. But of course I didn't know that then. On that day I was charmed and a little intimidated by talking to this pretty girl, just one year older than me, but really much older in some other sense.

I want to reach out to that boy. I want to warn him of what will come, I want to tell him to brace himself, to be strong. Instead, he will be blindsided, knocked silly. For years it will seem he has no direction, no true sense of himself. Crippled, he will walk among shadows, refusing to look back, turning away from those who caused him pain. He will believe that isolation brings safety, that distance alone brings healing. He will repeat the mistakes he once condemned in others. From such failures ought to come hard wisdom, but life is not always like that. If we want to redeem our past, to reclaim and reshape it, to probe the true sources of our deepest pain, we must make something wholly new. Little else can be done with the rubble.

The rain paused. It was time for me to go.

I wore my Glen Avon hockey jacket draped over my right shoulder like a toreador's cape, covering my cast and sling. Marta fastened the snaps over my chest. Then she stood before me, fingers gripping the collar of my jacket. She stood a good two inches taller than me. Feeling bold, I leaned forward for a kiss, touching my lips to hers. Her skin was cold and damp.

We walked home through my neighborhood. Lawns were bright green with new grass, the sidewalks shiny with rain water. Overhead, the boughs of birch and alder were swelling with tiny, delicate buds. Marta reached for my hand. We came to the intersection of Vermillion and Arrowhead Road. My house was a half-block away. I knew I was cutting it close. My mom was usually home by five on a Thursday. Sometimes she stopped at the grocery store to pick up something for dinner. If I hustled home right now, I had a chance.

Instead I asked Marta if she wanted to see where I'd had my bike accident. We walked another couple blocks to the foot of Grass Hill. We stood at the "T" formed where the sidewalk that continued along Vermillion met the long, straight, steeply-sloped sidewalk that ran down Grass Hill. I pointed up this foreboding promenade.

"This is it. I rode down here at, I don't know, thirty miles an hour or something." I pointed toward Sundby's house. "I jumped this curb, here, crossed the street, and hit that other curb as I was trying to stop." I felt a tingle of pride in my voice as I recited my saga yet again.

"Jackie Rose," she said, "you're the dumbest boy I ever met."

For one awful instant I froze. Was I humiliated? Ashamed? No, I was laughing. She was right! Of course she was right! No one knew it better than her.

"You're so dumb I love you," she said, laughing with me. "Come out after dinner and see me."

My mind reeled with the possibilities, but I knew it was impossible. My parents would never let me go out, not in a million years. And I wasn't yet bold enough to sneak out.

"Tomorrow after school, then."

"Maybe," I said. "I usually have to come home first."

"You don't have to do any of that!"

She leaned in close. I looked deep into her face. I wanted so badly to be with her, for her to take me on our next adventure. In her I sensed the raw urgency of a person willing to cross lines I'd never dreamed of crossing. But I was not yet that person.

"I have to go," I said.

A smile appeared in the corner of her mouth.

"I'll see you tomorrow after school. Don't forget."

We kissed somewhat stiffly and formally. I embraced her, felt her shivering in my arms. The drizzle had started back up. It was nearly dark and she had a long walk back to her apartment. I removed my hockey jacket and draped it over her shoulders. She thanked me, promising to return the jacket tomorrow. She kissed my cheek again, one last time, and was gone.

When I got home I found my mother sitting in the living room drinking coffee with Sharon Olsen, an old friend and the mother of Chris Cook, the boy I'd defended when I jumped Jerry Gustafson. (Sharon had divorced Chris's dad and remarried my hockey coach, of all people.) I hadn't seen Mrs. Olsen or her son since last summer. I was surprised, yes, and wary. Chris had changed schools due to the ceaseless bullying at Washburn. I'd been a part of that on both sides, but frankly with Chris gone it'd been easier for everyone to move on. Seeing Mrs. Olsen startled me. I felt a stab of guilt, compounding my intense unease at having been caught by my mother. But with Mrs. Olsen present I knew my mother would be polite, waiting to dissect me later.

"There you are," my mother said, smiling. "I've been wondering about you. Say hello to Sharon."

"Hi, Jackie." Mrs. Olsen had the sweetest smile. The lines around the corners of her eyes and mouth had grown more distinct since I'd last seen her.

She asked about my broken arm. (I gave her the stripped-down version, no heroics.) I knew my mother wanted me to ask about Chris, and part of me wanted to resist going there, but another part knew that an ounce of politeness now might spare me a pound of punishment later.

"How is Chris?"

"He's doing really well at his new school. They have a science club and he's in there every day after school. There's fifteen kids just like him, obsessed with rockets and chemistry and whatnot."

"Please tell him I said hello."

"Thank you. I'll do that."

"Now you go upstairs and clean up," my mother said. "You can wait for me in your room."

The look on her face was not warm. In my room I changed out of my wet jeans and shirt, fumbling with my one good hand for dry pants and a sweatshirt. I felt like a prisoner awaiting his sentence. And I had these Milk Duds and a *Motor Trend*, the cover now blistered with rainwater. What was I to do with them? I slid them under my dresser.

I heard my mother and Mrs. Olsen exchanging farewells at the door. It'd been too long, they said. They wouldn't wait so long before the next time.

"Never hesitate," Mrs. Olsen said. "Be brave, Ruth. You know you can call me anytime. I've been through it and then some. Don't let anyone shout you down."

Probably Mom's school plans, I thought. Dad was being such an asshole about it. Even I could see how wrong he was. Mom was doing great. There was no question she would go to college and get a degree. The only question was what would happen next.

But there were more immediate problems for me. Mere moments after the front door clicked shut, my bedroom door flew open. My mother demanded to know why I hadn't come home directly from school. And where was my coat? Don't think she hadn't seen me come in without it. And where had I been until well after five o'clock?

Farting around with John Skoglund, I said. I'd never once been late in coming home, honest, but today John and I had been tempted to do some lolly-gagging.

And where exactly had we been?

Walking along the creek, I said, zig-zagging the neighborhood.

"On a rainy day, for no good reason."

I nodded.

"And your coat?"

"Left it at John's. I'll get it tomorrow."

She stood there, arms crossed, with a big scowl on her face. Her momentary silence suggested that maybe, just maybe I was going to get away with it. But I should've known better.

"What if I told you that I called the Skoglunds to see if you were there, and John himself told me he had no idea where you were."

My throat suddenly felt as dry as sandpaper.

"Do you have anything you want to say?"

I swallowed.

The sniper's eye found its next target. Mom walked over to my dresser and extracted the *Motor Trend* and the box of Milk Duds perched atop it. She held the candy before me like a fresh kill.

"What's the rule?"

"No food in my room," I intoned, miserably.

She asked where I'd gotten the candy. I told her I'd bought it at Miller Hill drug store.

"Is that where you were today?"

"Yes."

"And how did you pay for it?"

"Piggy bank."

"And where is your coat?"

I froze, my mind empty of lies.

"I don't know." The stupidest answer, ensuring defeat.

She narrowed her eyes. "Are you ready to tell me the truth, young man?"

I was more than ready. Without a hint of redaction I delivered my story, blow-by-blow. I told her everything. Mom listened with a sober, stoic look on her face. If she was surprised that I had spent the day with a girl one year older than me—I said nothing of my previous adventures with Marta—she didn't show it.

After I'd finished she delivered a lecture on how disappointed she was, the violation of trust, and so on, at the conclusion of which she delivered her judgment. I was grounded every weekday from the minute I got home—and by God, I'd come straight home without so much as a step in the wrong direction—until bedtime, Monday through Friday, for one month.

That put me into early May, just about the time my cast would come off. Still a few weeks of school left.

Mom knelt before me, eyes wet. She was really upset about this, more than I'd thought. She put a hand to my cheek.

"I need you on my side," she said. "Don't turn away from your mother."

"I'm on your side," I said, quickly.

"See that you stay there."

She left me the car magazine but took the Milk Duds. I hadn't even opened them, never got to eat a single one.

8

With a broken arm the baseball tryouts were a moot point. I attended only to cheer on John Skoglund, who did what he had come to do with a calm and grace well beyond his years. I watched his every move with quiet envy. His prowess and authority in the batter's box were formidable for a kid our age, and he fielded fly balls and one-hop grounders with equal finesse. It came as no surprise when he got the call a week later, welcoming him to the Juniors. Congratulating him was much easier with a cast on my arm. It was understood that I would've been there, beside him, playing my heart out if it weren't for my injury.

It was a great cover. I worshipped that cast like a holy relic, knowing in my heart the pain and humiliation from which it had saved me.

With sports off the docket I turned to my books with redoubled zeal. In the public library I spent whole afternoons studying the incipient war. In books on Soviet military power I pored over the fold-out maps of western Europe. On the left side a slender line of blue dots coursed through eastern France and West Germany: NATO military bases and airfields. On the right side a sprawling mass of red dots extended from Berlin, Prague, and Budapest deep into central Russia. Any fool could see that there were twice as many red dots as there were blue. If a war were to break out red would swallow blue, no question. We stood no chance.

In other books, on other pages, voluminous charts and bar graphs confirmed the sobering truth. The Soviets outweighed us in nearly every category: number of ICBM launchers, home-defense SAMs, and submarine-based ballistic missiles; total throw-weight of land-based strategic systems; quantity of attack aircraft, tanks, and standing ground forces.

Only in the number of helicopters did NATO outstrip the Warsaw Pact. Helicopters! This seemed cold comfort.

I studied photos of Soviet mobile missile launchers crashing through Siberian forests, MIG fighter jets being readied on snow-covered airfields, the Red Army marching down Moscow's streets in an endless parade, their faces grim and joyless, focused on the task at hand: preparing to destroy the West.

The books frightened me so much I had to stop reading. I thought of what

Poindexter and I had discussed. I tried to imagine one young boy somewhere in the depths of Russia, curled up with a book and a broken arm, addled by fears larger than he could control, worried about a faceless, nameless West poised to destroy him the first chance it got. Who was this boy? Where was he? What was his name?

Things worsened around the house. At almost any moment, any time they were in each other's presence, my parents exploded into a huge row. They were long past arguing about school. They found new things. Money. How one looked at the other, or spoke. Where they'd been and with whom. When it started I was ordered upstairs to my room. Often I sat in the stairwell, around the turn and out of sight, eavesdropping, trying to figure out what was going on.

The bottom of my glass cries for whiskey. What I remember, and how much I care to piece together—

I am wrought with holes and gaps, I leak.

My mother asks where my father goes every night, what he's doing.
Dad says she knows where he is. He's out at the bars.
Bars close at two.
I'm home by then.
Sometimes, sometimes not. You were home at three on Tuesday. And four last night.
So I'm out driving around. Maybe I'm talking to somebody. Somebody who wants to hear what I have to say.
A drunk, you mean. Or somebody else?
You want to know the basic problem here? I am not loved or respected in my own home. A man should be treated with respect.
If you want respect, try earning it.
Maybe I do earn it. Maybe you're just not around to see it.
You want to tell me where you go to earn it? I'm dying to know.
What in hell are you talking about?
Why do you shower the minute you get home?
Bars make me smell like cigarettes.
Do they make you smell like Obsession?
What?
The perfume on your shirt collar. I don't wear it.

You accusing me of something?

Are you denying it?

You don't know anything.

What do I need, her panties? Don't lie to me, you son of a bitch!

Shut your damn mouth! He'll hear!

I don't care if he hears! He knows! He's not stupid!

Mom breaks down sobbing. They continue arguing, but I've heard enough. I creep upstairs, close my bedroom door, and turn on the radio. I crack open my latest tome, studying the stats on the Tupolev TU-26, the Russian "Backfire" bomber, capable of carrying thermonuclear weapons at Mach 1 for four thousand miles. I imagine a squadron of them rising above the horizon at dusk, coming in low over Lake Superior, their engines screaming like Valkyries, bomb doors open. We open our mouths to voice a futile scream as the first bombs tumble down. We might one day welcome it, the promise of a quick release.

I woke at three in the morning, startled by a bad dream. I wanted to know where my parents were. Their bedroom was empty. Downstairs the lights were on. My mother sat in the living room, awake, wrapped in a blanket and staring at the floor like she expected something to pop out of it. She turned to look at me when I walked into the room. She hard dark circles under her eyes. Used Kleenex littered the floor. But she wasn't crying.

"Where's Dad?"

"I don't know," she said, her voice cracked and rough. "But don't worry. Someone's taking care of him."

I wasn't sure what she meant. What perplexed me even more was the way she'd said it—with a hard, biting edge.

I told her I was scared.

"Don't be. I'm here. Your father is doing something he needs to do, I guess."

I took a few steps closer. "Are you okay?"

"I'm finished crying, I think." She offered a weak smile. "I don't want to shed any more tears for that man." She held her arms out. "Come here." We held each other in the dim light, her thread-worn blanket draped over her shoulders. She trembled gently and I pulled myself closer.

"Things are going to change," she told me, softly.

"Which things?"

"Lots of things." She explained that she and my father would soon separate.

I looked up at her. "A divorce?"

"No, not yet," she said, her mouth tight and drawn. "We're not quite there. We're going to try to fix this, Jackie. But, you see, we don't know how. Your father is going to move out of the house. We both need to think through some things, we both need space. We don't seem to be able to speak to each other without fighting."

I began to cry. I couldn't help it.

Sometimes adults disagree, she told me, but that doesn't mean they don't love each other. And I should never, not for one second, think that this had anything to do with me, or that it was my fault, or things would be better if I weren't around, or any of that.

"Both of your parents love you very deeply. You know that, don't you?"

Yes, I told her, I knew that.

My father had agreed to leave, she said. She and I would stay in the house. I'd see Dad often, could in fact visit him anytime I liked, and perhaps, before too long, he might even join us for meals. "But we'll just have to see how that goes."

"Where's he going?"

"He's got a room in a house downtown. Something temporary."

"Until...?"

My mother hugged me tightly. "Until we figure out the next step, is all. That's all I can say for now. We both need to clear our heads and ask ourselves what we really want. That's the only way I can put it, Jackie."

What we really want. That phrase resonated deep inside, like the sonorous blast of a fog horn bellowing over Lake Superior on a misty morning, calling into the haze, a sentry in search of a lost ship, a call begging for a response.

I felt something new, something strange, a feeling I didn't exactly understand at the time. Like something burning deep inside me, but icy. The way your toes or fingers burn after staying out for too long in the coldest weather, a resonant, needling pain that intensifies. I now understand: it was a kind of split or divide forming between me and the world, a new distance entering, just a sliver—but this sliver would grow to a wedge, then widen. The gap would never close, for I would never let it. I feel it even now.

It started there, in my mother's arms, as she spoke those words to me.

After my mother grounded me, I toed the line. That meant I saw less of John Skoglund and my other friends, including Marta. I came home straight from school and did my homework and chores. Then I watched a bit of television and snooped around (old habits die hard), but mostly I read.

On weekends I made trips to the library, taking out every book I could find on the Warsaw Pact, the NATO alliance, and the current state of military

154

strategies. This included a novel, *The Next World War*. The opening chapter staged a hypothetical Soviet invasion of western Europe. Massive Russian tanks ploughed through paper-thin NATO defenses. Meanwhile a volley of nuclear missiles took out Manchester and Brussels. We responded by torching Leningrad, and the game was on. In the novel it took the Soviets a mere six weeks to secure western Europe, which then became an impenetrable, continent-wide Communist fortress—dotted, of course, with the smoldering, radioactive remains of Lyons, Hamburg, and Naples. The book, written by a NATO general and a long list of "military consultants," confirmed my worst fears: the Soviet juggernaut, which so grossly outnumbered us, could crush us quickly, pressing us to their iron will.

I read the novel in a fervor, drunk with fear, before surrendering it to the library. Here is a story every man should know, I thought, a hard truth staring us in the face. Here is a last chance to act. The problem was what to do about any of it. The generals said we needed more bombs and missiles; President Carter said we needed less. They couldn't both be right. The whole thing seemed like an inscrutable mess.

In a few years it would be my generation's turn to tackle these questions. This was the mighty purpose of our education, or so we'd been lectured. Such thoughts flummoxed me, prompting new and deeper levels of disquiet. And if I didn't know exactly what we should do, I figured the first thing was to talk about it, to put it on the table, as my father liked to say. Always start with the facts.

Every student in Ms. Poindexter's sixth grade class had to deliver an oral report during the final weeks of the term, a ten-minute discussion of something you love, something you want to share with others. It was quite revealing. Who knew that Echo Lindstrom had a pet rat named Scamper? Eddie Gleason, who loved karate, tried and failed to split a plywood board with his bare fists. Jill McGilligan was an Irish dancer. John Skoglund explained the mysteries of the split-finger fastball, the slider, and the curve.

Marta Haugen, who'd missed a lot of school recently, was absent on the day she was scheduled to deliver her report. I've always wondered what she might have shared, what it would have taught me. She was always teaching me.

I, Jackie Rose, took a few minutes of everyone's day to explain an imminent threat facing us all: the looming specter of a Russian thermonuclear attack and the overwhelming odds that, should it come to war, the West stood little chance. I displayed my charts, my bar graphs, showed photos of towering mushroom clouds, glossy book illustrations of Russian warplanes and tanks.

I read a short passage from *The Next World War*, the one about the Russians incinerating Pittsburgh with a volley of ICBMs. Schools, churches, homes laid to waste. Nothing but a smoldering pile of radioactive rubble. Half a million dead.

I turned my questions to the room. Knowing this, do we want more weapons or less? Do we build more bomb shelters? Do we try diplomacy? *What are we going to do?*

The classroom fell silent. The faces of my peers were drawn, ghostly. Then a sniffle, a choked sob. Alison Miller wept into her hands.

"Jesus H. Christ," muttered Tommy Moore, a blasted look on his face.

"I say we nuke 'em first!" someone sang out.

"Thank you, Jackie," Ms. Poindexter said, frowning. "That was highly informative."

As she dismissed the class for lunch, she asked me to stay behind for a minute.

"Trouble again," said Echo.

"Teacher's pet," John muttered.

I didn't care what anyone said. I was intoxicated by the effect of my presentation. I hadn't anticipated such a powerful, uniform reaction. I hadn't been going for it, exactly. I'd merely sought to convey the urgency of my questions, to share the sensations I felt when I contemplated the impending war—the tingle of terror, the ecstasy of fear, what today I might call the erotics of imminent violence.

Poindexter scolded me, ever so gently, for frightening my peers. I'd been a bit melodramatic, if I knew what that word meant.

I knew. I muttered an apology, insincere and flat. I could sense this wasn't really what she wanted to say to me, and my hunch proved correct. She had good news to share: she'd been accepted into the education program at UCLA.

"Where's that?"

She smiled. "Los Angeles, California."

"You're moving to California?"

She nodded vigorously, a big grin on her face.

"When?"

"This summer. I thought you'd want to know. You remember this, Jackie. A girl from Duluth, who went to Washburn, and then to college, and then to Africa, and finally off to California for her doctorate in education. You can do anything if you put your mind to it and work hard enough. You remember that."

Yes, the familiar moral. I mumbled a congratulations. We hugged.

I walked out of the room to the enormous green doors at the end of the hallway and stepped outside, around the corner. I pressed my forehead against the cool stone wall and wept.

The cast came off the first week in May. I celebrated by taking a long, luxurious bubble bath without a plastic bag on my forearm, submerged in warm, soapy water up to my neck. Then Mom took me to Shakey's Pizza where I stuffed myself. She let me play two dollars' worth of pinball while she sat at the table reading another doorstop of a novel.

My arm looked a little funny at first. Gross, actually—flaky and pale. I swore my right forearm looked smaller than my left. I thought kids would call me Popeye, but Mom was smart and told me to wear long-sleeved shirts for a little bit and no one would notice.

Dad had been gone for a couple of weeks at that point. A strange yet satisfying calm had descended on the house in his absence. No more shouting matches, no more slammed doors. He'd taken his clothes on wire hangers, he'd taken his boxes of things. He'd taken his dirty magazines, which both dismayed and relieved me. And he'd taken the Pontiac, leaving us with no car.

My mother remedied that by purchasing a used '73 VW Squareback, orange, which she would drive for the next ten years until one day the engine literally fell out. (I would learn to drive in that car, with its silky-smooth, four-speed manual transmission.) Buying it changed our lives. Mom could now commute to campus quickly. No more mile-long walks or waiting for the bus in freezing weather. More importantly, she could get out and visit people. She could drive to dinner with a friend, or to the movies, or go shopping on a weekend. Separated from her husband, mother to a twelve-year-old boy, she could nevertheless leave home. Hers was a new kind of freedom.

My mother and I tried to keep brave faces for each other, but we were both pretty miserable. Mom cried a lot. In my father's absence a sort of funk hung over me. Despite the difficulty of living with him, despite the times I'd quietly cursed him and wished he'd leave, his departure left me feeling abandoned, unworthy and unloved. Our family was a failure and I was at the heart of it. I hoped and prayed that my parents could reconcile their differences, heal their wounds, and we could continue as a family.

Now I understand that my father's departure was long overdue and that my mother was poised to evolve in the most surprising of ways. It would take many years for these changes to manifest, and I chuckle now to think of who she'd be even five years later, when I was high school senior. I don't know who was harder to control.

Today I look back with kindness on my mother, who had the courage to re-invent herself, however messily. She applied to the college that spring and was accepted to begin as a full-time student in the fall. She decided she needed a job. She started waiting tables at a coffee shop downtown but that didn't pay well. By mid-summer she would get a job at a bookstore out on Woodland Avenue, on the same block as Marta's apartment. My mother would work there, part-time, for the next twenty years.

For my father, it was another matter entirely.

Marta never returned to Washburn Elementary. Naturally, rumors ran rampant. She'd flunked again. She'd been caught fighting, or stealing, or lying. She'd been sent to the Palmer School, or to juvie. The truth is no one knew where she'd gone, not even Carrie W.

One day after my cast was off and my curfew had expired, I walked over to the intersection of Oxford Street and Woodland Avenue. There was a row of shops—a hair salon, a small hardware store, and a flower shop. Further down the block was the bookstore where my mother would work, though she wasn't working there yet.

I walked up an external flight of stairs on the back of the building, leading to the apartments above. There were two mailboxes, one for a MacLeod and the other blank. A "Room for Rent" sign hung in the window. Inquire in the hair salon.

I asked the hairdresser when the Haugens had left and where they'd gone.

It'd been a couple of weeks. They'd left quite suddenly. No forwarding address. "If you find them, let me know. That lady owes me two months' rent."

I was sad to see Marta go. I wondered why she hadn't contacted me or Carrie or anyone. Not even Poindexter knew, or perhaps she wasn't allowed to say. I missed Marta's electric, daring presence in my life and I wondered at every opportunity I'd lost, all the strange adventures and touching we might have shared. She was a comet out of orbit, headed for some distant place, always several steps ahead of me. I wished I could keep up.

I never got my hockey jacket back. I hope she still has it, that she sees it and thinks of me, as I think of her. Today with social media it's easier than ever to find people. With a few clicks I can look at pictures of John Skoglund's kids, or read posts about Jill McGilligan's recent visit to Dublin. But I have never found Marta. She is truly lost, existing only in the memory I have constructed for her, sweet honeycomb of misery and exultation.

9

Though my father had the right to see me anytime he liked, we saw little of each other after he moved out. We spoke on the phone once or twice a week, but it felt awkward and forced. He asked how school was going, how my arm was doing. We bantered about the Twins' chances. The stuff acquaintances talk about.

One night, in a fit of despair, I complained to my mother. Dad didn't love me anymore. He hated me. It had been all my fault, etc. Tears and lamentation. My mother consoled me, as she always did, and promised to talk to my father.

A couple of days later I was informed that Dad would pick me up next Saturday at noon. We would spend the day together, just me and him.

Careful what you ask for.

My father picked me up on a spring afternoon in mid-May, one of the first warm days of the year. We drove with the Pontiac's windows down and radio playing, two guys with arms on the sill, enjoying the fresh air. That belied the ugly scene just ended. My parents had quarreled when my father arrived, picking up where they left off, snarling and hissing at each other. Nothing had changed, nothing.

"I'm sorry you have to hear all that, Jackie," my father said. "Your mother and I, we're just not suited for each other."

"You're going to get a divorce."

He shot me a cold look. "Did she say that?"

"No."

"I wouldn't be surprised if she did." He punched at the radio, changing channels. "I don't mind telling you, just for the record, she's the one who keeps bringing it up, not me."

We drove in silence for a couple of minutes. Then he asked me what I was reading. I rattled on about the Soviets, NATO, and our impending doom.

"Jesus," he said, "that's all you think about, huh? Next thing you'll go and join the army on me."

"I'd rather join the air force," I said. "I'd rather fly a jet."

"Your eyes aren't good enough."

"I have twenty-twenty vision."

"Combat pilots have better-than-perfect eyesight. And they're in top physical shape. Plus you have to know a lot of math and science, technical stuff. You better do well in school if you want to be a fighter pilot. You'll probably end up like me, changing oil and stacking boxes."

I almost said "Not on your life," but I held my tongue.

"I'm doing well in school."

"Good," he said. "Keep that up. I didn't do myself any favors back in the day. Study hard and think about doing something with your life. Get the hell out of this town."

"So you think college is okay?"

My father pursed his lips and took a deep breath, his eyes fixed on the road.

"Of course it's okay. You're going to finish high school and go straight in. It's best done when you're young, is all. Before you're all tied down with a job and a marriage and a kid."

"Couldn't you go back and get a degree?"

"What for."

"I don't know. But couldn't you?"

He was quiet for long moment before muttering, "There's no point now."

My father's answers angered me less for the cheap and predictable dig at my mother and more because they suggested he'd given up, perhaps had no ambitions to be anything other than what he was. It is one thing for fate to beat a man; it is quite another to see a man accept defeat, resigning himself to mediocrity. Though I couldn't have put it in words at the time, I felt the stirrings of a deep resentment inside me, a feeling I would come to know intimately. (I hate feeling it, I hate clinging to it, just a little more than I hate my father for inspiring it.) In years to come his comments—which I have never forgotten or, sadly, forgiven—would only resonate more fully, a pincushion into which I would insert many needles.

Ah, who is petty now? I offer this confession, with you as my witness.

He took me to a bar out on the Miller Trunk Highway, up in Duluth Heights, tucked between a car repair shop and a dry cleaners. It was smoky and dim and not even half full. Immediately after ordering two cheeseburger baskets with fries, my father handed me a mess of quarters and told me to go plug up the juke box and play a bit of pinball. He'd holler when our food was ready. Then he turned to the bartender, ordering a rye-and-ginger for himself and a root beer for the kid.

In the juke box I queued up "With a Little Luck," by Wings, and set about my first game of pinball. My arm was feeling stronger now, the last soreness from the injury fading. I took great pleasure in rocking and slamming that poor machine, angling my silver ball down the most lucrative chutes. The game proved forgiving; I never tilted.

Our burgers came and went. I barely touched mine—a lukewarm piece of roadkill, not even fit for the school cafeteria—though I devoured my fries, smothered in ketchup, without protest from my father. He handed me another pile of quarters. "Go on," he said, "plug that damn jukebox." He ordered himself another drink and got to talking to the bartender about something. My father had an easy, natural air about him. He could strike up a conversation with anyone about nearly anything. People wanted to be his friend.

Billy Joel, Captain & Tennille, Rupert Holmes: the songs came and went. I played "Cars" by Gary Numan three times in a row. I flipped through that day's *Duluth News-Tribune*, reading the comics and hunting for news of Russia. I lingered over an article about the ongoing mess with Mount St. Helen's, which was smoking like a furnace out in Washington State. In the past two months there had been a number of eruptions and hundreds of earthquakes. A plume of ash towered ten thousand feet overhead. Part of the mountain was swollen with magma, forming something called a cryptodome. A major eruption seemed imminent. Houses had been evacuated for miles around. Far away, spectators lined up to watch the eruptions and the magnificent lightning storms generated by the ash plume. But when, or if, the volcano might blow its top, the geologists could only speculate. Fat chance, I figured.

I tossed the paper aside, all of this only being a concern until the Russians nuked us and we went Day-Glo.

Several times I approached my father at the bar, tugging on his shirt sleeve. When were we leaving? He waved me off, calling for another round. Didn't I see he was busy catching up with Lou or Dick or whoever it was? He and the bartender were old pals, they hadn't seen each other in the longest time.

He said this without irony, without looking directly at me. He just kept handing me spare change, telling me to "Blow it, Jackie, blow it all! It's only money!"

Eventually I climbed into a booth near the front window, mindlessly watching traffic pour past on the trunk highway.

My father clapped a hand on my shoulder and announced in a loud voice that it was time to go. I followed him out the door into the blinding afternoon light. In the car my father fumbled with the keys, dropping them on the floor mat. He got it started, then floored the gas, making the engine roar.

"Listen to that baby," he said. "Four hundred and fifty-five cubic inches. This car may be old, Jackie, but she's still got some pep in her step. You can't count this old car out!"

Exiting the parking lot and turning onto the feeder road, he cut the turn too sharply. The back end of the car lurched up awkwardly. He cleared the curb and the entire rear end of the car came down with a terrific thud, followed by a long, grinding scrape of metal on cement.

"God damn it!" he shouted, jerking the transmission into Park and bounding out of the car, leaving the driver's side door open. From the dash came a soft, steady pinging sound, the chiming of a caged bird. My father crouched down along the rear quarter panel of the car, cursing and spitting in the dust. When he returned his face was red and his right forearm was streaked with dirt. He put the car in gear and accelerated quickly, running a stop sign at the end of the feeder road and darting into traffic on the trunk highway, talking loudly as he drove.

"I don't need this bullshit! She thinks I asked for this! I didn't ask for anything! And I can God damn sure as hell take it or leave it!"

Hearing this disturbed me less because of what he said—it seemed innocuous—than because it was in the tight, high voice he used when he was talking to himself in the basement. It was a voice he used when he was alone, when he was angry, and at that moment I wondered if he even registered that I was in the car with him.

My father drove up the trunk highway, past the mall, out to the airport. When he rolled through the departure area, weaving between the haphazardly-parked cars, their trunks yawning open, luggage scattered all over as travelers hugged and waved farewell, I knew my father had no plan, no goal or direction. He was just driving for its own sake. Finally we left the airport and headed back into town. But then he took a left turn into Duluth Heights, across from the mall. He drove up and down the hills in that neighborhood, around the curvy roads until I lost track of where we were. Apparently my father had nothing better to do than drive around aimlessly; I was stuck with him until he cooled off.

We pulled up outside of a yellow house on a steep incline. I remember my father cranking the steering wheel to his left and stepping down on the parking brake with a satisfying crunch. The house was built into this steep hill so that the left side appeared partially submerged, as if a tide of dirt and rock had poured around it. We walked up the driveway. There was a low brick wall along its left side, weeping moisture onto the asphalt in tiny rivulets.

My father rapped on the white screen door in a quick, percussive rhythm. The front door of the house was open, admitting the warm spring air. "Lorraine," he said once, loudly, and then he surprised me by opening the screen door and stepping inside. He beckoned me to follow.

A voice came from inside the house. "Carl, is that you?"

I entered and found myself on a landing between two floors. The stale smell of cigarettes hit me. Upstairs was a living room with white shag carpet and a green armchair. A row of tall plate glass looked out onto a stand of evergreen pine. The room had a somber look to it. Downstairs I saw a basement of some kind, dark and sepulchral.

A short woman in white culottes and a yellow satin blouse emerged from the hallway upstairs, her brown hair arranged in a messy bun. She stood at the top of the stairs, cocked a hip, and took a drag on her cigarette.

"I can't wait to hear you explain this."

"We were in the neighborhood," my father said.

"Sure you were." She turned her gaze to me. "You must be Jackie."

"Yes, Ma'am." My throat felt tight.

"I'm Lorraine, a friend of your father's."

I mustered a nod. This woman did not seem unkind. She had a small face and round cheeks, like a child's. She wore lipstick and eyeliner, as if she were going out.

"Your cast is off," she said. Her knowing that unnerved me; I knew nothing about her.

My father climbed the steps up to the main floor, one hand on the metal railing. "Jackie's going to go downstairs and take a look at your television while we talk," he said, a little loudly. He walked directly past this woman, this Lorraine, disappearing down a hallway to the right. "I'd like a drink."

"As if you need one."

She hadn't taken her eye off me. Her gaze, steady and calm, betrayed not the least bit of disturbance. She knew my father well, that was clear. I wondered why she lived in such a dark house, and if she liked it that way.

"You want something to eat, Jackie?"

I shook my head.

"I guess I'll talk to your father for a bit." We heard the clink of glass bottles in another room. She turned her head in his direction. "Has he been driving you all over town, sauced like that?"

Of course I knew my father drank, and I'd gathered from my mother that his drinking was a problem. Yet I'd never heard anyone outside of our immediate family comment on it. Her statement embarrassed me. What could I say to that?

Lorraine took a long drag on her cigarette, slowly exhaling, a gray cloud swirling around her like a serpent. "You go on downstairs," she said. "My ex-husband has quite a collection of books. I know you like to read." She strode silently down the hallway.

The basement was one long rectangular room with a wall of bookshelves on one side and, facing it, a pair of cabinets flanking an all-in-one television and stereo unit. I scanned the bookshelves—fat paperbacks by Michener and Uris, plus a whole mess of Don Pendleton's Executioner series—before moving to the picture window, looking out onto a steeply-pitched back lawn. In one corner of the yard stood an aluminum-hulled fishing boat turned upside-down on blocks. I studied the royal blue stripe along the hull, interrupted by the state license decal. Its tags were current.

I understood then that Lorraine was only recently divorced. Where had her ex-husband gone, I wondered, and why had he left his things behind?

A floorboard groaned overhead. I heard muffled voices through the heating duct. Lorraine said, sharply, "Well I just can't. Not with your son downstairs. What do you think you're doing, anyway, bringing him here?"

I moved to the stereo, lifting the lid on the cabinet to access the turntable and an eight-track tape player. Linda Ronstadt's *Simple Dreams* was jammed in the mouth of the machine. Funny, my dad owned the same tape, playing it frequently in his car. I remembered a day, a couple months back, when Mom had asked me to bring it in. She was dying to hear "Blue Bayou." I went out to the car and rifled through Dad's collection, which he kept in an old shoe box. The tape wasn't there. Later, when I asked him about it, he said he'd lost it.

I pulled the tape out of the machine. Sure enough, there were his initials on the back, "CR." (He initialed all his tapes and albums.) It bothered me that the tape was there, but I was even more bothered by the fact that my father had lied to me about it. It suggested other, perhaps greater deceits. I don't know how long I stood there, staring at the strange object in my hand, clutching it like an artifact from a lost religion. Finding it meant we were all infidels.

Upstairs, Lorraine shrieked. "Get your hands off me! Don't you dare touch me like that!"

A door slammed. I heard my father's footsteps clomping down the hallway.

"Come on, Jackie, it was a mistake to come here," he said, loudly. "I've screwed this thing up, too."

I hesitated, tape in hand, unsure what to do. I couldn't bring it to the car. I only knew I didn't want it being played for this Lorraine, whoever she was. I dropped it behind the heavy blue sofa against the back wall and ran to catch up with my father.

Outside the sky was darkening. The temperature had dropped. The promise of a spring storm hovered in the air. My father walked quickly across the front lawn, his gait heavy, arms swinging in long, ape-like movements.

The screen door shot open behind us. Lorraine stepped out, barefoot on the flagstones of her porch, her face twisted in a frown.

"Carl, be careful! You have your son in the car!"

"Don't worry your pretty little head about it."

My father wrenched the driver's door of the Pontiac open and all but threw himself behind the wheel. I climbed in beside him. Before I even had the door shut he was revving the engine. He dropped the car into gear and we sped forward, motor roaring. I felt the back end slip and catch, the tire spinning, and when I looked behind I saw that he'd torn up a strip of grass along the side of the road, spraying dirt and gravel behind us. The car lurched up the steep street and my father cut a corner sharply, veering into the opposite lane. Then we were racing downhill, my father sitting forward, his face red and eyes narrowed, white knuckles gripping the wheel. Frightened, I reached for the seat belt, which I almost never wore, and clutched the door handle.

We came to an abrupt halt at a traffic light. Before us cars streamed along the Miller Trunk Highway.

"Tell me where you want to go," he said. "Anywhere. You decide. Do you want another drink? We could stop back at that armpit of a bar. I'll buy you all the soda you want."

I swallowed, my throat tight and dry. "Why don't we just go home?"

"That's the one place we can't go."

"Can you drop me off?"

My father turned to look at me, his brow low and tight. "Don't want to be around your old man, either, huh?" He turned his eye back to the street. "If I get within a hundred feet of your mother there's no telling what I might do."

"Do you hate her that much?"

He released his grip on the steering wheel, fingers extended stiff and straight like knives, then regripped the wheel.

"It's not hate," he said. "No matter what your mother tells you, Jackie, I do not hate her. The problem with your mother is she doesn't know how to love."

That statement didn't seem true or fair—in fact it seemed outrageous, even offensive—but it was obvious my father was in no mood for a debate. The light turned green and he accelerated into the intersection. We were heading back into the city. Thankfully he drove the speed limit, chugging along in the right-hand lane.

"We'll go to Canal Park," he announced. "Maybe we'll have a look at that new museum. I hear it's worth a visit."

This was his attempt at mollifying me. My sixth grade class had taken a field trip to the Duluth Maritime Museum a few weeks back. I'd loved it, and delivered an enthusiastic report to the dinner table. Dad had scoffed at the idea. Canal Park would always be a dump. My mother told him to hush. Things can change, she insisted.

We rode the Trunk Highway to Central Entrance, crossed Arlington Avenue, and then down the hill and into the heart of downtown. Below us the lake stretched out, a black void under the slate-gray skies. A stout maroon ore boat chugged into open water, its bow stiff and erect, proudly plowing the chop. I wondered where that boat was headed, what its sailors were thinking, and if they were glad to be leaving everything they knew on land behind.

We rolled down the cascading tiers of Lake Avenue to the bottom of the hill and entered Canal Park, in those days a slightly seedy warehouse district with a strip of shops clustered around the aerial lift bridge. My father parked and then turned off the car but made no move to exit. The engine ticked softly.

The parking lot was half-empty. I studied the aerial lift bridge. Its two iron-trellised towers stood on either side of the ship canal, with a single span of roadway between them that could be lifted to allow for the freighters and ore boats that came into the harbor. It was a fascinating machine, a skein of intricate metal scaffolding and beams, every bit as lovely as the Eiffel Tower.

My father lowered his head to the steering wheel. "I don't know what to do."

Before us, in the small park surrounding the Maritime museum, a toddler careened down a grassy hillock. A mother stood at the foot of the hill, arms extended, ready to catch him.

"Let's get out and walk around," I said.

My father did not immediately respond. I thought maybe he'd fallen asleep. But then he sat up, took a deep breath, and agreed. I got out of the car first. The sky had darkened further, the clouds low and gray. The stiff onshore breeze was downright cold, and I wished I had a windbreaker. Out over the lake I could see heavier clouds moving inland. Only a matter of time, I knew, before whatever was coming would hit us.

We walked out along the west pier of the ship canal, a long concrete embankment with a squat lighthouse at its end, like a giant's severed thumb. At the end of the pier I climbed the concrete steps up to the foot of the stumpy white lighthouse. The iron door was secured with an enormous metal padlock. Graffiti covered the tower's sides. Empty beer cans littered the promenade. I walked around it to the very tip of the pier, leaning against the cold concrete embankment. The lake stretched out before me, blue-black. White-caps crashed and collapsed atop one another, one after the other, expending themselves onto the pebble beach. Gulls hovered head-on in the shore breeze, their sharp, barking calls a desperate rhythm all their own.

My father stood beside me, stiff and erect, facing the breeze which blew his hair back. "There are things I want to tell you," he said, "but you're only twelve, Jackie, you're only twelve. One day, a few years from now, maybe I can tell you. I want you to know that I love you. Your mother loves you. No matter what happens, don't forget that."

His words frightened and confused me. "What's going to happen?"

He spoke in a trembling voice. "You can want something so bad that it hurts. And at the same time, once you have it, you can only think about getting away from it. It'll drive you crazy, the back-and-forth in your head. After a while nothing makes sense."

I dug my hands deep into the pockets of my jeans. "What are you talking about?"

"I'm leaving."

"Going where?"

"California." He cleared his throat. "I haven't told your mother. You're the first to know. I wanted you to be the first."

Something in his voice, the hardness and certainty with which he spoke, convinced me this was no bluff. Tears welled, but I fought to keep them back.

He knelt beside me and put a hand on my shoulder. "I want you to come with me. It could be us, just the two of us." The look on his face in that instant, so boyish and open and tender, alarmed me. "We could leave right now, Jackie. Just hop in the Pontiac and head west. It'd be an adventure!" He cracked a feeble smile. "I'll be better, I promise. Better than ever."

"Dad, Dad." I didn't know what else to say.

His grip on my shoulder tightened. "Tell me, what do you think? Just you and me." The look in his eyes demanded an answer.

"No," I said. "I'll never leave Mom."

He lowered his head. His fingers pumped my shoulder once, twice, and then fell. We stood like that, a father kneeling as if in penitence before a son too young to offer absolution. I wish I could keep him there, forever begging my attention.

Finally he stood. "My son," he muttered. "Christ, what am I doing." He began walking back along the pier. I hesitated, letting him walk on alone.

* * *

My father waited for me on a bench near the museum. I sat beside him, arms folded across my chest. We were quiet for a very long time, watching the parade of families strolling up and down the embankment on a breezy Saturday afternoon. He asked again if there was anything I wanted to do. I pointed to the small observation area on the span of the lift bridge. I'd always wanted to ride on it.

He nodded. "Let's go see about that."

We inquired in the museum. The bridge was scheduled to lift within the half-hour. An ore boat, the *Charles Henry Bellingham*, was shipping out. My father bought tickets and we walked onto the pedestrian portion of the bridge. The floor of the aerial lift bridge's span is an iron grate; beneath us rushed the cold, black water of the ship canal. The tires of the cars and trucks crossing the bridge created a sonorous, droning hum. In the center of the bridge stood a small cage made of cyclone fencing pressed up against the iron balustrades. At its entrance a small queue had formed. A man collected tickets, counting heads out loud. I handed him mine and stepped inside. Only then did it register that my father had purchased just one ticket. He wouldn't join me, for whatever reason. I was through asking why.

The metal door clanged shut and the attendant locked it. After a series of horns and bells the central span of the bridge magically rose, quiet and smooth. Up and up we climbed, higher and higher. The span slowed and came to a rest, nestled against the arch of the bridge. We hung there, suspended two hundred feet in the air. To my left the city of Duluth clung to its hill overlooking the lake, the tightly-packed downtown surrounded by rings of homes. At its feet the jagged, rocky shore, lined with bluffs and stout boulders. From there the enormous blue-black lake spread out, seemingly to infinity. I shivered in the icy onshore breeze, mercilessly slicing through my T-shirt. My knees felt watery. I had never been that high before, suspended over the dark and indifferent water. A fall from this height would surely kill me, the coldness below swallowing me without remorse.

Beneath us, the bow of a maroon ore boat entered the canal, the clean white steering house followed by long rows of cargo holds, and then the stumpy rear quarters. A lone sailor in a blue denim shirt and jeans stood astern, one foot lifted onto the iron rail, smoking a cigarette. I waved to him and he returned the gesture with one slow, solemn chop of the hand. I studied the ship's wake, the churning copper-brown water disturbed by massive, unseen forces.

I lifted my eyes, searching for my father. I found him in the center of the small green, sitting alone on a wooden bench, head in hands. And as I watched he stood, threw his arms out, and began to walk toward the parking lot where he climbed into his Pontiac.

Cold, I thought.

Brake lights flashed. The car backed out of its slot. It rested a moment before pulling forward, moving to the nearest exit. Going, going, gone.

I wrapped my fingers around the wire of the cage, gripping the cold metal. *My father, my father, what have you done?* It seems impossible, even now.

Then the bells rang out, gears began to turn, and the bridge lowered silently, terribly back into place.

In the divorce proceedings which quickly followed, my mother was awarded full custody. My father ceded everything but his cash and his car, leaving us the house and his belongings, all the things he left behind. He headed west, not to California but to Alaska, where he bounced between air bases before settling in at Eielson, servicing the jets of the 354th Fighter Wing.

I visited him once when I was sixteen, spending a rather glum couple of weeks in his bungalow, hiding from mosquitoes. When he had a little time off we drove up to Fairbanks for dinner. One weekend we rented a boat and went fishing on the Chena River, casting for grayling and chum salmon. In mid-summer the sky is light all night. We fished until one in the morning, my father drunk on cheap beer. Our catch was small. He promised to take me up to Denali the next weekend, but then he got an offer to cover an extra shift. Desperate for money, he said he had to take it.

He drove me the next day to the Fairbanks airport. We embraced stiffly. I'd come with a long list of grievances and accusations, but in two weeks I hadn't gotten within a mile of it. The thaw had barely started; I don't know who was more stubborn about it, him or me. We parted without tears or speeches. That was Sunday, July 22nd, 1984, the last time I saw my father.

We would talk on the phone in years to come, though it tapered off after I entered college, distracted by girls and my studies, in that order. I continued to play ice hockey, one topic we could discuss with shared enthusiasm. It was a club sport at Carleton. I played right defense, fighting my way out of the corner, clearing the zone and defending the net as always.

When my father died I realized we had not spoken in over five years. I cannot say I knew the man well. And while my mother and I have spent many an hour dissecting the past, I never heard my father's version, not that he would have cared to share it. But I would have liked at least to ask. I would have liked to hear him speak his mind to me as an adult, as one more capable of understanding. But I never asked.

And so it is memory I cling to, these memories to which I return like the bright notes of a song, an old record dropping onto the turntable, the needle descending to its scratchy groove. The first notes call back an era, playing through it one more time until it reaches the final spiral, a locked groove where the needle bounces in place, mindlessly repeating itself until a gentle finger reaches over to lift it, freeing it from time.

Acknowledgments

I am grateful to the Fulbright U.S. Scholar Program and to California State University, Chico for their support of my creative endeavors.

Three sentences in "Infidels" have been borrowed, with utmost affection, from Paul Bowles's story "Pages from Cold Point" (*Collected Stories 1939-1976*. Santa Rosa, CA: Black Sparrow, 1994).